D0263152

georgie

malachy doyle

First published in Great Britain in 2001
Bloomsbury Publishing Plc, 38 Soho Square, London, W1V 3HB

A CIP catalogue record of this book is available from the British Library

ISBN 0 7475 5154 5

Printed in Great Britain by Clays Ltd, St Ives plc

10 9 8 7 6 5 4 3 2 1

For Penny

2 april

'Are you awake, Georgie?'

I open one eye. It's Ruby, with my breakfast.

They're not supposed to do that, come into my room. It's not safe.

'I've something to tell you, love,' she says. 'OK?'

I nod, just. But I don't like it. Don't like things different. It makes me nervous. They're supposed to leave the tray outside. Supposed to knock on the door, say 'Morning, Georgie. Here's your breakfast,' and go.

I'm not nice in the morning, that's why. I'm never nice.

I watch Ruby with my one open eye. She edges in a bit further, holding the tray out in front of her. To protect her, I suppose.

'You're going to a new home, Georgie,' she says. 'A new home in Wales.'

She watches me. I don't blink, don't move.

'It's Sally's school. Remember Sally who came to see you last week? She's lovely, and the school sounds great. You'll have your own room, all done up specially for you, and you'll have new friends, lots of new friends. You're going to be happy there, Georgie, happier than you've been in a long while. And I'm really looking forward to coming to visit you . . . '

She's talking too much. Too fast.

'But I'm going to miss you, Georgie,' she carries on, smiling the fakest smile I've ever seen. 'We're all going to miss you . . . '

Yeah, sure. I open the other eye, give her one of my death stares, one of my if-you-say-another-word-you're-finished sort of looks. And it works. It always works.

The words dry in her mouth. Her bottom lip hangs open and then it closes, slowly. I watch her face tighten, her body go stiff. Hands shaking, she puts the tray down on the end of the bed and glances over her shoulder at the half-open door. There's someone outside. Waiting, keeping guard, in case it goes badly.

It's going badly.

But Ruby doesn't give up, that's one thing I'll say about her. Carries on to the bitter end, every time. So she has another go, even though she knows I'm about to lose it. She has another go, desperate to get the whole of her message across before I'm so out of it I won't even be able to hear what she's saying.

'We're leaving tomorrow morning, in the minibus,' she goes on, voice cracking. 'You, me and Keith. I'm sorry I couldn't tell you earlier, love, but I didn't want you to get upset.'

You didn't want me to get upset! Oh, that's nice of you, isn't it, Ruby? I'm gritting my teeth now, and she knows I'm about to blow. I can see the fear in her eyes, smell the sweat on her body. She's afraid to stay, because she can tell something bad's about to happen. But she's even more afraid to run, because she knows that if she does I'll hate her for it, hate her for ever.

'You'll be able to make a fresh start, Georgie,' she cries, almost pleading. Her voice is rising, squeaking. 'It's what you need, you know it's what you need. A clean sheet. A chance to begin again. A chance to be normal.'

Normal! What the hell does that mean? I throw back the covers and Ruby finally realises she's gone too far. That it's time to run.

She backs out of the room fast, slamming the door behind her.

I reach for my tea. Cold, always cold. I drink it anyway, and everything is white, white and angry. My fingers tighten on the plastic handle and I squeeze till it digs into my skin. Then I fling the mug at the door. Another stain, trickling down the paintwork. Another stain to add to all the others.

No way. No way am I leaving here. This is my home.

Some home. A mattress on a bare floor. Because that's all I've got left. All I've got left in the whole world.

I wreck everything, that's why. Everything they give me, everything I ever owned. I rip it, break it or piss on it.

I go out on the landing when everyone's gone. I make sure Molly cleaner's not around. She hates me, does Molly cleaner. Hates me to hell and back.

I sit on the toilet, pushing it all into my hand, and then I paint the walls brown. Brown to wash out the white of my anger. Brown to make them hate me. Oh, how they hate me.

Back in my room, I tear off my pyjamas and rip them to shreds.

I run to the window and thump it till my fist's sore.

I grab hold of the radiator and I pull it, pull it. I'll have it off the wall one of these days, and then there'll be a right bloody mess.

When I've done enough damage, I stop. When I've burnt out my anger, I stop. When I'm tired and empty, I push the mattress up against the door and sit in the corner. Naked, cold, dirty.

Leave me alone. I want to be alone. I'm a nasty, horrible boy and I don't want anyone near me.

later

Ruby comes back up before she goes off duty. She brings me water, a towel, new pyjamas, in case I want to clean myself up. I want to clean myself up.

When she returns, I let her in. She's OK, Ruby. She used to safen me when I was smaller, when I came here first. Her long, dark hair was my hiding place from the outside world. Whenever I got nervous or frightened or lonely she'd wrap me up in it, and I'd snuggle in her warmth, in her darkness, until I was calm.

But those days are gone, long gone. I scare her now. I'm too big, too strong.

She's still frightened because of the way I looked at her this morning. She tries to pretend she isn't but the fear's still there – in her sweaty skin, her whining voice. Pleading, she is, pleading to be forgiven.

How can I forgive you, Ruby? How can I possibly forgive you? I trusted you, Ruby, and look what you've done! You're kicking me out of my room, my home. You're sending me away from everything and everyone I know.

You tricked me, Ruby, tricked me into liking you, tricked me into thinking you cared about me, tricked me into thinking you were here for ever, that I was here for ever.

Yes, you tricked me, Ruby, and if there's one thing I can't stand, it's being tricked.

When she comes within reach I grab her. At first it's only meant to be a warning, a sharp little tug and away. But I'm pulling and pulling, I'm lost in her darkness and the anger's rising. I can feel it in my guts, all queasy, like diarrhoea. Spreading into my chest, pounding, pounding. Up to my throat, the taste of vomit. And then the rage, the uncontrollable rage fires all around my body – my toes twitching to kick, my fingers becoming fists, my skin, the whole of my skin, raw.

You won't protect me, Ruby, from the world, from myself. I used to think you loved me, Ruby.

Now I know you hate me. Because you're sending me away, you cow. From everything that's safe. You're sending me away, you bitch, from everything I know.

When she screams, I jerk away. A clump of her dark, glossy hair stays in my hand, ripped by the roots from the top of her head.

She screams and screams and it only makes me even madder. You fear me, I hurt you. You hate me, I hate you. Fear, hate, what else is there?

Keith comes rushing in and I lash out again, nails flashing. Ruby's cowering, trying to cover herself up so I can't attack her, but I seek out the gaps between her gentle fingers and gouge the side of her face. Nasty, sharp, never-cut nails on her soft, soft skin.

Blood. Blood on the whiteness of my anger. Blood on my hands and I freeze. Keith grabs me and pulls me off her. Roughly, too roughly. That's how it is with Keith.

But it's too late anyway. For me, for Ruby. It's always too late.

The door slams behind them and they're gone. Leaving only me, a mattress and a cold, empty room.

3 april

'Morning, Georgie. Here's your breakfast.'

A voice. Bright and cheerful.

Piss off! I don't want your brightness. I don't want your lies, your pretence, your trickery. Just piss off, all of you, and leave me alone!

I wait till whoever it is has gone, and then I climb out of bed and open the door.

There's a tray with the usual – soggy cereal, cold tea. But there's a pile of clothes too. I look away. I don't want to see them. They're someone else's clothes, not mine. They're new clothes.

I haven't been dressed for three months. Haven't been downstairs for four. It grew so that every time I went down I lost it, so I stopped. At first they used to come and get me, but that only made it worse. Dragging me down, kicking and screaming. Upsetting them, upsetting me, upsetting the other children. What good was that to anyone? So they gave up.

I pull the tray inside, slam the door on the clothes so I don't have to think about them, and then I eat the food. I always eat the food. There's no point starving, is there?

There's a card by the bowl. A boy and a dinosaur. The boy's waving, smiling. Inside I can see lots of writing, lots of names. I can't read the words but I know what they mean. It's obvious, isn't it?

Ruby's right. They're sending me away.

When they come up I'm dressed in the stiff new clothes. I hate those clothes, almost as much as I hate myself. It makes me sick to the stomach to put them on. Sick to the stomach to feel them touching my skin. But there's no choice. I'm bad. I'm bad and I have to go.

Because that's what happens. That's what happens when you're a Georgie. You can fight and fight but, let's face it, you're never going to win. You can kick and bite and yell and scream, but it never does you any good. In the end they're the ones that decide what happens. The adults. The ones with the power. They make all the decisions and when they tell you to go, you go.

I avoid their eyes. I always avoid people's eyes. But I walk down with them, because there's no choice. Slowly, sideways, with Ruby holding both my hands so I can't lash out. There's no kids around, of course. They've learnt to avoid me, learnt to keep out of my way.

When we get to the bottom of the stairs, Ruby lets go one hand to unlock the back door. As she opens it, a blast of cold air hits me. A blast of outside air that I haven't felt in months. It's freezing, like the ice in my head, like the whiteness in my heart.

And suddenly I can't do it. I can't face starting all over again. I know there's no other way, of course. I know I won't win no matter how hard I fight, no matter how hard I bite, because they've got the power and I've got nothing.

I know it's all I deserve, anyway. It's my punishment for being bad. And yet I still can't do it. I won't do it. I back up on the stairs, grab the post, bury my head in my arms and sink inside myself.

Ruby's gone out to open up the bus, so that only leaves Keith to sort it out.

'It's OK, Georgie,' he says, crouching down next to me. 'You're doing fine.'

It's not OK, though. And I'm not doing fine.

I don't like Keith. He's the one they always call when I lose it. Hissing at me through his teeth, threats that no one else can hear. Grabbing me too roughly, holding me too tightly. No one else seems to notice, but I know what he's about. I know how much he hates me, hates this job, hates himself. I know what he can do when the others aren't looking.

I'm bad and I've failed again. I was trying so hard, doing so well. I wouldn't talk, of course, I never talk, but apart from that everything was OK.

I'd eat with the others, ride on the bus, go to school every morning. And they were pleased with me. Everyone was pleased with me. Even I was pleased with me.

Till that stupid boy came. The one with the big teeth. I don't know where they found him, what hell-hole they dragged him up from, but he appeared one morning, all butter wouldn't melt in his mouth, all slimy smile. I took one look at him and I could tell there was going to be trouble.

They put him in my class, on my table, and they should have known it wouldn't work. Someone should've known.

He didn't like me, right from the start. I didn't much like him either, but I wasn't planning to do anything about it. Other than pretend he wasn't there.

But he was there all right. Slap bang in front of me, and he was going to make damn sure I was aware of it. He stared at me, hissed at me, and I ignored him. He pinched me, kicked me, and I ignored him. He spat at me, swore at me under his breath, and I ignored it. And no one noticed. No one cared.

And then he grabbed my book, my animal book, and started tearing out the pages. Slowly, slowly, one by one, holding the book out in front of me and ripping each page from top to bottom. Watching my face to see how I'd react. And that was it. I couldn't ignore him any longer.

I looked up into his eyes. I gave him a death

stare to end all death stares. And he ignored it. Smiling at me, that evil smile of his, as he carried on ripping out the pages, tearing them from top to bottom.

As I reached across to grab the book back, he sank his teeth into my arm. The pain shot through me and I snapped, I finally snapped. I jumped to my feet, pushing over my chair, and came flying round to his side of the table. I hit him and hit him until blood poured from his face. I hit him and hit him until my hands were red. It took three of them to pull us apart.

Everyone blamed it on me, of course. Picking on the poor little new boy. Because no one had seen what that evil little bastard had been doing. Winding me up, tighter and tighter, loving every minute of it. Because no one cared. Because no one had even bothered to look.

And I couldn't tell them, of course. That's the worst thing about not speaking – you can never explain, never get people to understand.

I couldn't tell them he'd been asking for it, begging for it. Pushing me and pushing me until I cracked.

So I stopped going to school. Why should I, if that blood-sucking monster was going to be there? Why should I, if no one cared about me anyway? Why should I, if all they were going to do was blame me every time something went wrong?

They'd try to get me on the bus and I'd fight and kick. I'd throw myself on the ground and refuse to move. I'd lie there, biting my wrists so hard they'd bleed. Biting anyone else if they came too close.

So in the end they'd have to leave without me. I'd stay in the houseroom all day, doing nothing. And whoever had to stay behind to look after me would make it pretty obvious they were fed up, too. Fed up with having to stay behind in a boring room with a nasty, horrible Georgie.

So I took it one stage further and stopped even going downstairs. I wouldn't get out of bed, wouldn't get dressed, wouldn't come down for breakfast.

Because the more you do, the more they expect you to do. And the more they expect you to do, the more you disappoint them. So I stopped doing anything at all. And they gave up on me completely.

And now they're sending me away. Away to a new

place, new people. It's only natural, I suppose. You can't really blame them. It's what anybody with any sense would do, get rid of me. I mean, who'd want all this hassle, anyway?

There's just one problem. I don't want to go. I really, strongly don't want to go.

It's not up to me, of course. I've no choice. No voice. They've got the power and I've got nothing.

I could make any amount of fuss, but it wouldn't do me any good. I know that, really. I'm the loser, in the end. Always the loser.

I stand up. Put my hands in Keith's. Breathe deeply. Walk out the door.

We climb into the bus. I sit in the back against the window, where I used to sit. Keith's next to me, holding my hands tightly. Ruby's in front, her long, brown hair hanging down the back of the seat.

Stupid, that. Asking for trouble. Why do they never learn?

Dave turns round and smiles. He starts the engine and everyone appears outside the house: Justin, Zeta, Ragga, everybody. Smiling and waving, just like the boy with the dinosaur. Rest of the staff too, they're all there. Even Molly cleaner and she hates me.

They're all acting as though it's a special day, a happy day. A day to sing and cheer and wave flags. A new-queen sort of a day. An end of the war sort of a day. We won and Georgie lost. Whoopee!

Philip the boss climbs into the bus and shakes my hand. 'Goodbye, Georgie,' he says. 'And good luck! You're a grand lad, you know.'

Yeah, sure. Easy to say that now he's rid of me.

And then, when he's gone to join the others, off we go, down the drive, through the gates and away. Away for ever.

I'm glad Keith's got my hands. I don't like him, I don't like the way he holds me. Tightly, too tightly. I don't like the way he whispers through his teeth, warning me to behave. But at least it stops me from doing anything I shouldn't.

I force my eyes closed, pretending to sleep. Safer that way. Stay cool, Georgie. You can handle it. Don't look at the road, the road that's taking you away. Don't look at Ruby's hair.

Don't think about your stomach, either. Your

stomach turning, churning.

Oh, god, I think I'm going to be sick.

later

'Wake up, Georgie, we're here.'

I know we're here. We wouldn't have stopped if we weren't here. What do you think I am, thick? Why do you always treat me as though I'm thick?

Keith tightens his grip on my hands again, just in case I blow. Funny how it scares and settles me all at the same time, the way he does it.

I open my eyes. It takes them a while to adjust to the light.

A big grey building, alone. A woman comes out. Walks down the steps, past some yellow flowers, over to the bus. I remember her now. It's Sally. She's tall and thin and she's got long, dark hair. Why does everyone have long, dark hair?

'Hello, Georgie,' she says. 'Welcome to your new home.'

I avoid her eyes and hold on to Keith. I don't want a new home, you stupid cow! Don't want a new anything. I just want to go back to my room, my old room, and hide from the world, the world outside, the world that wants me to be someone I'm not.

But there's no going back, of course. I know there's no going back. I've lost Ruby, lost my room, and I'm starting again with nothing.

I want to fight but there's no fight left in me. I want to scream and rage, to bite and kick, but I know I won't win. Keith will pin me down till it hurts. Sally will be disappointed, and I'll have failed already.

So I hold hands and we follow her in. Through the big wooden doors, into the main hallway, up the winding stairs, along a corridor.

There's kids all over the place, just doing what they're doing. Watching me. Not watching me. No one's told them who I am. No one's told them to hide. No one's prepared them for what's about to hit them.

'Here's your room, Georgie,' says Sally, opening a door at the end of the corridor. 'We've done it up specially for you. I hope you like it.'

Keith gasps. So do I. It's got a proper bed, a chest of drawers, wardrobe, pictures. There's even a stereo! And then I see the mirror. A full-length mirror, made of glass, real, breakable glass.

Is that Georgie staring out at me? Is that what he looks like now? Pale skin, dark eyes, lost. I turn away from him. I don't want to see him, I don't want him to see me.

They must be crazy, giving me all these things. Don't they know? Don't they know who Georgie is? Don't they know what he does to things?

It's quiet now. I stand by the window. Everyone else has gone, and I can see flowers. Trees. Sheep on a hillside.

I take off my shoes and sit down on the bed. I'm tired. So tired. I tried to sleep on the bus, but I couldn't. I tried to sleep last night, but I couldn't.

I hate the nights. I'm alone in the day, but I'm even more alone in the night. And it's stupid, so bloody stupid, because I spend all my life in my bedroom and yet I never sleep. Not at night, not properly.

I dream, that's the trouble. If I sleep, I dream. If I dream, I see knives. If I dream, I see blood squirting, pouring, gushing all around me. It makes me wake, screaming. It's the only time I use my voice any more – to scream.

You'd think they'd notice. Me, who never says a word, screaming the house down. You'd think they'd hear me from miles away. You'd think they'd drop everything and come running to see what was the matter. To see how they could help me.

All I want is someone, anyone, to come and put their arms around me. To tell me it's just a bad dream. To tell me it's all right.

But it's not all right. And no one comes. The night staff leave me, shivering, alone. They turn up the radio to block out the sound of my screams.

Maybe they think I'm some sort of monster, and as soon as they open my door I'm going to come flying at them with an iron bar, smash them to a bloody pulp.

No. There's too much blood already. Every time I close my eyes they fill with blood. Every time I try to sleep I can taste it in my throat, I'm choking on it till I can't breathe. Choking on it till I wake, crying out for someone to come, someone to care.

So here I am in my new room, my lovely, frightening room. I climb in under the duvet, curl up in a ball. Close my eyes on all the things they've given me. Because I know what they mean.

Crawl out of your shell, Georgie boy, that's what they mean. It's time to become a human being, that's what they mean. Act normal and we'll treat you normal.

But I can't. It hurts too much. Don't they know how much it hurts, trying to be normal, trying to be human? You think things you don't want to think. You feel things you don't want to feel. You open up your mind and remember things you don't want to remember, things no one should remember. Things you've slammed the door on, things that never happened . . .

So I close my eyes. Tight. Tight. Close myself down, way down, beyond now, beyond memory. Close myself down, so far down that I actually manage to sleep. Deeper than dreams, deeper than nightmares, almost deeper than life itself.

I sleep. For once, I sleep.

later

Later, some time later, they come to say goodbye. They give me time to drag myself out of the hiding place of sleep, to remember where I am, what's happening. Then Keith shakes my hand, and I let him. Ruby gives me a hug, and I let her. I don't hug her back, of course, but I don't push her away, either.

And they're gone. Gone from my life. Ruby says she'll be back in a few weeks to see how I'm getting on, but I know she won't. They never do.

I lie on my bed and I'm sad. Sad because I've lost Ruby.

But I'm glad too. Glad because I'm rid of Keith.

I'm sad, though, because I'm in a strange place, a place I don't know.

Yet I'm glad as well, because it really is a lovely room. And it's mine, all mine.

Most of all, though, I'm sad. Sad because I know it won't stay lovely. Sad because Georgie wrecks things.

There's a knock on the door and it's Sally. A man with her, a tall man. Beard. Jacket.

'This is Tommo,' says Sally, smiling. 'He's going to be your teacher.'

I look away. Who cares? I've had it with teachers. Had it with men, too. They've too much strength, and even if they don't mean to, they always end up using it. So I ignore the man, the teacher man.

But out of the corner of my eye I watch him as he moves round the room. Out of the corner of my ear I listen as he speaks. If he's going to try and be my teacher, I need to know what he's like. Need to know what he's going to do. Because teachers have power. Special power. You need to watch them closely.

He moves OK, doesn't come too near, doesn't force himself on me. Speaks OK too, I suppose. With a soft voice, quiet, calm. I'm not too bothered about the words, I'm not really taking them in, but he's talking quietly about this and that, and he's got a funny singsong voice, a bit like music. When's the last time I heard music?

Sally tries to slip away without me noticing, but I see her. I see the little smile she gives Tommo when she thinks I'm not looking, and I wonder if they're playing tricks on me. They'd better not be. I don't like tricks.

Just me and the man. Me lying on my bed, him sitting in the chair.

'It's a nice room, Georgie,' he says. I look round, and I know he's right. But it's a strange room, too – a scary room, full of beautiful things. It's too good for Georgie, really.

Tommo sits by the window. He's stopped talking now and he's looking out, humming a tune. It's a funny thing, humming. It's not something I ever do, ever remember doing. It's not something people often do around me, either. Maybe it only happens when you're calm. Maybe music only bubbles up out of you when you're happy.

He's not like all the others, this Tommo man. He's quiet, for one thing. Doesn't fill all the spaces with words. He's big enough, strong enough, to worry me, but for some reason his strength doesn't scare me at all. It sort of makes me feel safe.

And you can tell he feels safe with me, too. Safe from all the things I could do if I didn't like him. The sort of things people who don't like Georgie expect me to do.

Like, he doesn't expect me to grab his beard and pull it off his face. Doesn't expect me to jump out of bed, wrench a picture off the wall and crash it over his head, either. He doesn't expect me to run across the room and put my fist through the window. Or kick at the full-length mirror and send splinters of glass crashing all around us. Oh, no, he doesn't expect any of that. None of them do – that's why they've given me this room.

So I won't. I won't do any of those things. Not now, anyway. Not yet.

I sit up, and Tommo starts to talk again. Quietly, almost as though I'm not there. This time I find myself listening more closely. Listening to the words as well as the music. He talks about his wife, his children, the things he likes doing.

Smiles every now and then, but sort of quietly,

almost to himself. Not the big showy pretend smile some people do that's supposed to put me at ease but always ends up winding me tight as a fist. Not the timid, forced, twisted little smile others do that makes me know they're terrified of me. His is a real smile, an honest smile. I catch it sideways, because, like I said, I don't look at people straight on. But there's something about him that makes me want to look back. That almost makes me want to smile in return.

He rummages about in his bag and pulls out a few things. One of them is a book of photos, photos of the school. He asks me if I want a look. Draws his chair a bit closer. I pretend I'm not interested, pretend I don't care what other kids get up to, but I do really.

The thing is, I'm not that different, you know. Deep down, I'm not that different. I might not talk, or read or write. I might not leave my room, I might have pale skin and a hollow face, dark eyes and sores on my wrists where I bite them, over and over so they never heal, but I'm not that different, really. So I cast a glance at the photos, every now and again. To see what other children do.

They go swimming here, he says, turning the pages. Gardening. Cooking. They walk in the hills, the ones I can see from my window. It looks OK in the photos. They look happy.

Wish I could be happy. Just for once. Try it out. See what it feels like.

They play games too, he says. Chasing games, touching games. I couldn't. Not me, not with the others. I've seen them, some of them, on my way in, my way upstairs. I can see them in the photos. They're a bit odd, a bit scary.

But there's a girl. About my age. Red hair. Smiling at the camera. Cheeky grin.

'That's Shannon,' says Tommo. 'She's in my class. I think you might like her. She's quite a character, is Shannon.'

Tommo stays. Brings up my dinner. Pulls a sandwich out of his bag and asks if he can eat it.

I don't eat with other people. Haven't for months, or is it years? I've lost track of time. Lost track of how long it is since I did the sort of simple, everyday things that make you human.

I shake my head at him. No, no, you can't! No

one eats here, no one but me. And then I hold my breath. Wait to see what happens. Men don't like being told what to do, what not to do.

'Fair enough, Georgie,' he says and shrugs his shoulders. 'It's your room. You make the rules.' Then he slips the sandwich back into his bag.

'Tell you what,' he says, putting all the other things away too, 'I'll pop up to the staff room for a while and have it there. Is that all right?'

I nod, surprised.

'I'll see you later then,' he says, and he's gone.

later

He's gone and he's left one of his books behind. It's on the floor, by the chair. I wonder if he meant to. He didn't say.

I lean out of my bed, looking at it. It's got a picture of a bird on the cover. A bird with its wings spread wide, flying through the air. I like birds.

I lean further out and I'm that bird. Wheeling,

diving, soaring through the clouds. I'm that bird, free.

I want to pick the book up, to look at it more closely. I like books, or at least I used to. When I was little, before it all went wrong. Books about bears, I liked. Books about animals. I knew how to read once. Some of the words, anyway. Before everything changed, before it all slipped away.

I want to turn the pages, to look at all the birds inside, but I'm afraid to. Afraid in case I spoil it. Afraid in case I tear out the pages, rip off the wings so the beautiful birds can't fly. That's the sort of thing a Georgie does.

Someone's watching me. It's that other Georgie, the one in the mirror. I look up and there he is, spying on me.

'Go on,' he says. 'Destroy it.'

Why did Tommo leave the book here, anyway? Is it a trick, to tempt me?

And why did they put me in this room, this room full of so many things? This room where I can never hide because Georgie's always there, always watching, always on at me to do things I shouldn't, always expecting the worst?

I turn my back on the other Georgie, turn my back on the book. I pull the duvet over my head and hide, hide from everything. It's not fair. I'm not ready for all of this.

But my mind keeps being drawn back, back to the beauty of the birds, their freedom. I climb out of bed and pick up the book, slowly, carefully. I turn the pages, gently.

It's all right, you beautiful birds. I won't harm you. I promise I won't harm you.

Show me how to fly. Show me how to sing, you beautiful birds.

There's a noise on the landing. Someone's coming. My hands shake, the book slips from my grasp and hits the floor hard. They'll hear me, they'll see me with it, they'll think I stole it.

I jump out of bed and kick it in underneath so no one can find it. It'll be broken now, all bent and broken.

And there's Tommo at the door, smiling. 'I'm off home now, Georgie,' he says. 'I wondered how you liked the book?'

He sees my face, ashamed. Sees my eyes glancing

to the floor, under the bed. 'I'm sorry, Georgie,' he says. 'Didn't you like it? Do you want me to take it back?'

He reaches in to pick it up, and I'm standing above him, angry. It's all his fault, for leaving the book here in the first place. It's all his fault for tempting me, tricking me. I could kick him, I could kick him hard. I could pull my foot back and slam it into his ribs.

But I don't. The moment passes and he's back out again, with the book in his hands. And it's not bent, not broken. It's not even dirty.

As he holds it out to me, I avoid his eyes, afraid he might see my anger and how near I came to hurting him. I take the book, though, and press it close to my chest.

'Oh, Georgie!' he says. 'I'm silly sometimes. I should have just given it to you. I wanted you to have it, as a present, but I wasn't sure if you'd accept it. So I just left it there on the floor for you to find. I wanted it to be a surprise for you, but all it did was confuse you.'

He looks at me more closely. 'I can see that you like it, though. Do you want to keep it?'

Slowly I nod my head yes.

'Good,' says Tommo. 'It's yours, then. You can read it here in your room.' He smiles as he turns to go. 'And if you feel like coming to school some time, once you've settled in and all that, maybe you could bring it with you.'

After he's gone, I climb into bed with my book. There's a bit of dust on the cover, but I blow it off, into the air. Then I open up the pages and look at the birds. And they can still sing, still fly.

You're mine, beautiful birds! All mine, Tommo said.

He said something about school, too. Something about going over to school some time. But I'm not going to bother about that. Not going to worry about it. Not now.

I turn another page and something drops out on the floor. I reach down to pick it up and it's the photo of Shannon. The one that Tommo was showing me. How did that get there?

Red hair. Cheeky grin. Quite a character.

I look at it closely. Then I slip it back in between the pages, close the book carefully and put it on the table by my bed.

later

It's dark outside. I'm standing by the window with the light off, watching the darkness settle in all around me. I've been standing here for hours, just me, the silence and the growing darkness.

Suddenly the door opens and an old woman barges in with my medicine. I spin round, eyes flashing. Couldn't you wait? Couldn't you at least knock?

I see the fear on her face and I'm angry, so angry. Because she's scared already, scared before she's even met me.

Someone must have told her. Told her what Georgie's like, what he does to people. So much for the clean sheet. So much for the chance to start again.

There's a smell of fear on her, bitter like piss. She comes over to give me my medicine. Touches my arm. No!

Short, grey hair in thin little curls clinging tightly to her head. Nothing to really get a hold of, but I grab it anyway. It's not that I want to hurt her, not really. No, I want to lift up her hair and crawl inside, hide from my anger, hide from myself, hide from the me that makes people afraid. But you can't hide behind someone who's afraid of you, you can't ever hide in short, grey hair. All you can do is pull, pull hard.

She screams, drops the plastic tray and tries to run from the room, but I won't let her go. I can't let her go. As the liquid runs down my duvet, everything's anger-white, inside my head and out. My fingers are tangled in her curls, and I can't shake them free. She's pulling to get away and it only tightens my grip. There's a tearing sound, a screaming sound.

The door slams and the old woman's gone. Gone and my mouth is full of the horrible, bitter taste of failure. Gone and my fingers are full of her hair.

I shake my hand to get rid of her nasty grey curls and they fall on my rug, my beautiful rug. They fall on my bed too, into the sticky liquid. I try to brush them off, but they cling to my hand, cling to the duvet.

It's spoilt, everything's spoilt. My bed, my rug, my room, my new home. All spoilt because there's no more hair to hide in. All spoilt because of some stupid cow who's been listening to people slagging me off, some ignorant old bag who hasn't a clue, who doesn't understand that she shouldn't come barging into my room, that I need my privacy, my silence. Some stupid, narrow-minded bitch who doesn't realise that I've come here to start again, that I need to be given another chance.

All spoilt, too, because of a nasty, horrible boy watching me in the mirror. A nasty, horrible Georgie boy who won't let me go. Won't let me grow.

I lash out at the rug, kick it in under the bed where I can't see it, can't tear it into tiny pieces. Tear my duvet off my bed, my sticky, horrible duvet. I shove it in after the rug. Under the bed, out of sight.

My eyes dart around the room. They rest on the mirror again, on Georgie. I'm going to smash you, Georgie boy. I'm going to smash your ugly face into a thousand million pieces.

Stop! Don't do it, Georgie. Don't listen to the noises in your head filling the world with anger. Don't listen to the voice in the mirror drawing you deeper, deeper into failure.

It doesn't have to be like this, Georgie. It really doesn't have to be like this. Sit in your chair by the window. Look at the darkness falling. Look at the flowers and the trees and the sheep disappear.

Breathe slowly, Georgie. Breathe gently.

I'm sorry, old woman. I'm sorry I hurt you.

I want to be good. Please let me be good, someone. Please let me.

shannon

The new boy came today. Georgie, he's called. I saw him getting off the bus. I'd sneaked out of class and I was up in my room, watching.

He was scared. I could see it in his eyes, in the way he moved. He's the same age as me, Tommo says, but he looked much younger, the way he was holding hands with that guy who brought him in. Holding both hands, so he had to walk sideways, like a crab.

I'm not surprised he was frightened, though. Who wouldn't be? I remember the day I arrived, I was scared shitless. Of this big old house in the middle of nowhere, of the people inside it. The kids were bad enough – society's rejects, the ones that no one wanted. But somehow I got it into my head the place was haunted, too. Sad, I know, but as I stepped out of the minibus this massive shiver ran all the way down my spine. It took me weeks to stop feeling cold, weeks to stop tiptoeing around the place, peering into corners, looking for ghosts. I'd lie in bed at night and think I could hear them crawling around in the room above me. I'd stare into the dark and imagine them in my room, at the end of my bed, coming closer, closer.

I'd throw on my light and there'd be nothing there, of course. Just a stupid teenager, spooked by squeaky floorboards, rattling windows, that sort of thing. I'd never lived in an old house before; I never knew how they moan and groan.

Every now and again I'd hear screaming too, of course. But I was used to that. Some kids just scream.

It grows on you, this place. Full of weirdos, yeah, but you get used to them. Especially if you're weird yourself. They don't half wind you up, mind, but I know it's not their fault, so I go easy on them. Most of the time, anyway.

I still lose my cool every now and then, if someone tries to push me around, say. But it's not often. Most of them know what I'm like by now, so they keep out of my way when I'm on the edge. Or when they are.

The staff are OK, too. Most of them, anyway. Most of the time. Some are a bit wet – the old ones, the new ones. They back off too easily, the wet ones, don't hang on in there with you when things are bad. They think they're being kind to you by giving you space, but they're not really. They're scared, I reckon. Scared of getting their hands dirty. Scared of getting involved.

But there's no thugs, no bullies. No one who gets off on having power over kids who can't answer back. Not on the staff. Not here. Which is saying something, after the places I've been. The things I've seen.

Yeah, we're messed up, every one of us. Problem kids, they call us, but I've been thinking about that. There's a lot of time for thinking, round here. And it's not us that's the problem, that's what I've come to realise. It's the adults. The ones out there, the ones that are supposed to look after us and don't. The bastards who mess up their own lives and then take it out on their kids. They're the problem.

They're the ones who made us like we are.

They're the ones to blame, if anyone is. And it's them that should be locked up, not us, not the victims.

I've started writing it down. That's what this book's about. It was Tommo's idea, he's the one that suggested it. Whenever he saw me about to blow a fuse, when everyone else was running for cover, he'd come over. I'd curse and swear and go ballistic, throwing my arms around, kicking things, you know how you do, and he'd just sit there, waiting. And then, when I'd calmed down a bit, enough to notice what was going on around me, enough to hear what he was saying, he'd be talking, quietly. About this and that.

Interesting stuff, though. Stuff I'd want to hear, after a bit. So he'd talk and I'd listen, and eventually he'd get me to join in. About this. About that. Not about what was bothering me, not the real reasons anyway. I wasn't ready for that. I wasn't ready to let anyone inside my head. But I'd be skirting around the edges. Touching it. Backing off. Touching again.

And then one day he pulled out a pen and paper

and handed it to me, saying, 'Write it down, Shannon. See if you can put it into words. Not for me or anyone else. Just for yourself.'

So I took it. Just to get him off my case. Not actually meaning to do what he said. But I was sitting there with the pen in my hand, and somehow I found myself writing. And writing.

And it's funny, but it worked. You wouldn't think it would, but it did. All the things I couldn't say, all the thoughts that it was too painful, too embarrassing to tell anyone. I found I could write them.

I wrote like crazy that day, writing out my anger. I wrote so hard it tore the paper. I damned them all to hell, all those people in the past, for what they'd done, for what they hadn't done.

I wrote and I wrote and when I'd finished writing I looked up. The sun hadn't fled from the sky, the other children hadn't turned into monsters. Everyone else was getting on with their own thing and the world was still turning.

The next day Tommo brought me this book and said, 'Why not keep a diary, Shannon? A diary of your thoughts. Write something down every day.'

So I did. I wrote about what I was feeling, about where I was coming from. Sometimes just simple things, the things I'd done that day. Sometimes horrible things, things I'd never dared to even think about, never mind put into words.

It dragged me down, the writing, deep down into myself, deep down into the past where I didn't want to go. Deep down where I was cut off from everyone around me. It took me over after a while, so that all that was left on the outside was my anger.

It pushed everyone away. It made me so edgy, so touchy, so damn dangerous that it forced them all back. First the children and then even the staff. They couldn't understand why I'd changed. Why I'd gone from the cold, nervous Shannon I was when I first arrived to this crazy woman.

Everyone pulled away. Everyone except Tommo. Because he understood, because he knew what was happening, knew what I was going through. He hung on in there with me, believed in me.

In time I showed him some of what I wrote – not at first, of course, not while it was still so raw, but in time, when I was ready. We began to talk then, talk about real things, things that mattered. And the mist began to clear.

I wonder if that'll happen with Georgie. He looks as if he's had some hard times, that kid. I wonder what he's like inside, behind the damage.

Tommo says he's going to be in our class, if he can get him over. Says he hasn't been to school in months, which is part of the reason they sent him here.

Says he can't read or write. Says he won't even talk. Hasn't for years. I don't know why, though. Don't know if he can and won't, or just can't. I asked Tommo, but he wouldn't say. I'm not sure if he knew himself.

'Bet you I can get him talking,' I said, laughing.

Tommo smiled. 'No chance, Shannon,' he said. 'With you around, no one gets a word in edgeways.'

I went down the stairs as Georgie was coming up. I'm not supposed to be on the boys' stairs, of course, but no one said anything. They were too busy sorting him out even to notice me, you could see. Sally was doing her 'Welcome to Abernant, we'll take good care of you' bit, but I could tell she was nervous. Three staff with him, he had. One of them, a man, was holding him too tight. A thug, he was – you could see it in his eyes. Georgie's well rid of him.

Mind you, he's been running rings around them, has Georgie. You can tell that too. I tried to catch his eye, but there was nothing there. Shut down. Lost to the world. Totally out if it.

I know a bit about that. I know how it happens.

So you've hit rock bottom, kid. Reached the end of the line. Abernant's where they send you when they've run out of ideas, when there's nowhere left to try. They take you as far west as they can without dropping you off the edge, and they wave goodbye. Leaving you there, hanging on by your fingertips to what's left of your life.

And the funny thing is, it's not so bad. You think it's going to be a complete and utter disaster and it isn't. Or at least it wasn't for me. You see, by the time I landed up here I was so pissed off with being pissed off, I was just about ready to make a change. It took me a while to see it, but when I did, with a bit of help from Tommo and the writing, it was like BAM!

What he helped me to do, when the time was right, like I said, was to open up all the doors into my past and take a long, hard look. For three, four weeks I let it all rise to the surface, all the crap that had happened to me. For three, four weeks I felt like shit – crazy, clear off my head. No one could get near me. No one but Tommo.

I was raging – at God, at my folks, at everyone I'd ever come across. Why me? Why did it have to be me?

And then suddenly, one day, I put it away. I said, Right, Shannon, you lived it once, you've just relived it, now what? You can wallow in it for ever, all this shit, or you can pick yourself up and get a life.

I can still remember one of the things Tommo said. He said, 'You've been blaming yourself, Shannon. All these years you've been blaming yourself for what other people did to you, and it's *not your fault.*'

It took me a while to see it, to really believe it, but when I did, it changed things completely. 'You've lost five, ten good years because of what they did to you,' he said, 'because of what they didn't do. They've ruined your childhood, girl. Are you going to let them ruin the rest of your life, too?'

No way! No bloody way!

So what about you, Georgie? Are you ready to open up the past and take a long, hard look at it, too? Because if you're anything like me, and I've this funny feeling you are, then that's what you've got to do. It'll do your head in, I can promise you that, but it's worth it. It's worth it in the end.

Well, it worked for me, anyway.

4 april

It's cold in the night.

I pull my duvet back out from under the bed. It's still a bit sticky, because of the medicine, but at least it's warm. Feathery, soft. Why make a fuss, Georgie? Why do you always make a fuss?

I curl up tight and think about the good things, about flowers, about birds. I close my eyes and I sink, sink into the pillow.

I sleep and I don't dream. Sleep and I don't scream. Sleep and I wake up to sunlight streaming in through my window and the gentle sound of someone tapping on the door.

A woman, a different one, with fair hair. She pops her head round the door and asks if I want breakfast. Smiles.

I let her bring it in and put it on the table. I wait till she's left the room and then I get out of bed.

The tea's warm. The cereal's not soggy. I eat it

quickly, and when everyone's gone down, I go out into the corridor to have a wash.

As I'm coming out of the bathroom, I see a flash of red hair. Someone's running down the stairs. I duck back inside and wait till it's quiet again. I'm not ready to meet anyone. Not yet.

When I get back to my room, I find a piece of paper that's been pushed under the door. It's blank, so I turn it over. There's a smile, a face smiling. And underneath it there's two wavy lines.

I don't know what the wavy lines mean, but someone's sending me a smile. Wanting me to be happy. I wonder who. Why?

I hide it under my pillow. Then I find my clothes and wait for the man. The teacher man, the Tommo man.

He comes at half past eight. I know what time it is because he brings a watch and shows me. Lets me hold it.

He stays with me for a long time. Sometimes he talks, sometimes he just sits, looking out of the window. I like that. He doesn't push.

He doesn't seem to mind that I'm strange. Doesn't mind that I'm quiet. He's quiet too, I suppose. Maybe that's why he's OK with me. Not quiet tight, like me, though. He's quiet easy. Quiet happy.

When he leaves, I go to pass him back the watch, the beautiful watch. I've been holding it in my hand, the cool face of it pressed into my palm. Counting away the minutes, the seconds, beating gently against my skin.

'No,' he says, and I catch his eyes twinkling. 'It's for you, Georgie. You can keep it.'

When he's gone, I stand by the window, looking at the sheep on the mountain. It feels good.

I turn to Georgie, who's looking at me from inside the mirror, and this strange feeling bubbles up from my toes. A giddy sort of feeling. Next thing I find myself wiggling my hips, grinning like an idiot, sticking out my tongue at him.

I've got a smiley face and you haven't!

I've got a bird book and you haven't!

I've got a beautiful watch and you haven't!

I've got a room full of things I like, I haven't wrecked them yet, and you've got nothing!

Because I'm here, and things are changing. And

you're in there, behind the glass, the same old Georgie, stuck in the past.

I stop then. It doesn't feel quite right, doing all that happy stuff. It doesn't feel like it's me. Some day, maybe some day it will be. But not yet. I'm not ready yet. Not on my own, I'm not.

I press the watch up against my ear again and listen to the tiny tiny ticking. I pull out the smiley face, and I smile in return.

shannon

Georgie didn't come to school today, but then I didn't think he would. Not yet.

I listened in to the staff, like I do (I'm a brilliant eavesdropper, me), and I heard he had a go at that new woman, Anne, last night. I'm not surprised, really. She hasn't quite got the hang of it yet.

They shouldn't have sent her up on her own, mind. Short-staffed, I suppose. The usual problem. It's always the same, everywhere I've been. There's never enough staff, the new ones are thrown in at the deep end, and then people wonder why things go wrong. It's not fair, you know. It's not fair on them, and it's certainly not fair on us.

Wonder if there'll be any sign of Georgie at the weekend. Wonder if he got my message. I'd like to see him again, but I don't suppose I will. Not for a good while. I don't think he's ready to come out of his room yet, never mind anything else. He'll be hurting too much, like I was when I first got here. Hurting too much to let anyone near him.

That's what happens. They move you here, they move you there, one dump after another, and in the end you stop letting anyone get close because you know it'll all end in tears. The only person you like, the one you thought really cared about you, goes and gets another job, and it's back to square bloody one.

Or you're the one that has to go – they move you to a new home, spin you all sorts of fairy tales about how it's the ideal place and you'll be so much better there, how everyone there's really looking forward to you arriving, and how everyone here's going to miss you oh so very very much and they'll be queueing up to come and visit you just as soon as you've settled in blah bloody blah. And what they really mean – and you damn well know it, and they damn well know you know it, so why don't they stop coming out with all this social worker crap and tell you the truth, for Christ's sake? – is they can't stand the sight of you one second longer. You're a pain in the neck, you have been for years, and the sooner they wash their hands of you, the sooner they can palm you off on somebody else, the better. Then they'll put you clean out of their minds and within a day or two it'll feel as if you never even existed.

So that's it. You have to start all over again. But the trouble is, you can't be bothered any more. Love hurts, so you give up on it. You put up the shutters, push everyone away, and become someone no one can love.

Take it easy, Georgie. Give them a chance and you'll find out they're different here. They're not just after an easy life. They care. I know it's hard to believe but they actually care. Some more than others, of course, but it's there and it's for real.

Give it time, give them time to get to know you, and you'll feel it, like I felt it. That strength they've got. A strength you can draw on. The strength you need to make a change.

You can do it, Georgie. I know you can do it.

I bet Tommo comes in to see him. Bet you he tries to get him talking before I do. He likes a challenge, does Tommo. Thinks he can work magic with kids like us. The weird thing is, he can, sort of.

I'm going into town tomorrow. That's good. Shake off the others for a while and wander round the shops. Act like a teenager. Pretend I'm normal.

Best bit of the week.

5 april

I wake up this morning and there's another smiley man under my door. More wavy lines underneath. They're good. I like whoever's drawing them, sending them.

Straight after breakfast Tommo appears. I've been waiting for him. Hoping he'll come.

'It's Saturday,' he says. 'There's no school today, Georgie. I don't really work weekends, as a rule, but I thought I'd just pop in to see how you're getting on.'

I peep into his eyes, his deep blue eyes. I glance past, and in, and away again. It's the best I can do. The best I've done in a long while. But I like Tommo. I like what I see.

I'm wondering if it's him who's sending me the smiles. It doesn't feel like it's him. It's not the sort of thing he'd do. And they arrive too early, anyway, before he's even got to school, don't they? I wish I could ask him straight out, but I can't, of course. I could take one of them out from under the pillow and show it to him, see how he reacts, I suppose. But in a funny sort of way I don't really want to. Because I want to think it's someone else, not him. I want to be able to think I've got two people who care about me.

It's a secret. My secret. I don't remember ever having a secret before. Not a good secret. Not one I shared with someone else.

I'm glad Tommo came, even though it's Saturday.

'How would you like a walk round the grounds?' he says. 'Just you and me.'

I look up in surprise, in alarm. Go for a walk? Where? How?

I climb back into bed and pull the covers all around me. All my pleasure at seeing him has gone, slipped away, just like that.

Don't push me! Everyone's always pushing me, too hard, too fast. Making me do things I don't want to do. Not leaving it up to me to decide.

I'm angry at Tommo now. I thought he'd understand. I thought he'd know better.

But I'm cross at myself too. More than I am at him, really. I'm cross at myself for feeling like this. For not being able to go along with it. For not being more normal.

Calm down, Georgie. Breathe slowly. Breathe deeply.

Silence, though I know he hasn't left the room. Silence, and then a rustling sound. I peep out from under the duvet and he's holding a newspaper. He's sitting in a chair by the window, reading.

'Take your time, Georgie,' he says, as though it doesn't matter either way. 'It's up to you.'

I'm breathing slowly. Trying to calm down. Trying to work out what I feel.

I still feel cross, cross that he would even ask me. Surely he knows I don't do that sort of thing. Surely he knows I need to be in control. To take things at my own pace, in my own time.

But I feel relieved, too. Relieved that he's just sitting there, reading a paper, instead of piling on the pressure. Relieved that it doesn't seem to matter to him too much. No one's ever done that before – sat in my room doing a crossword or whatever it is he's up to. No one would dare.

Mind you, shouldn't I be cross about that too? Doesn't it mean he's not taking me seriously? Doesn't it mean he's just playing games with me? Trying to trick me?

Five minutes pass. 'I'm just going down to get a cup of coffee,' he says, putting his paper down. 'Do you want me to get you anything?'

I don't answer.

I wait till he's gone and I climb out of bed. It's a lovely day. I look at the sheep on the hillside. The fields, the trees, the sun, the sky. And suddenly I realise that even though it was his idea first, I want to be out there, in the open. That, as long as it's my decision, not Tommo's, then this is a good time to do it. And Tommo's a good person to do it with.

Because I'm so fed up with rooms, with walls, with the smell of stale air and sadness, stale air and disappointment. I'm so fed up with being on my own.

I find my clothes, my new clothes, and put them on. I hear Ruby inside my head. It's a fresh start, she's saying. A chance to start again.

OK, Tommo, let's go for it.

'You're coming? Great!' says Tommo when he comes back up and sees me dressed. I can see the surprise on his face, but he covers it quickly. 'Give me a couple of minutes to drink this, and I'll be right with you.'

I wait. I almost laugh. Me all set to go out, waiting for someone else. That makes a change.

We go down the stairs. There's a girl in the hallway, smiling at me. A girl with red hair, dungarees, a cheeky grin. It's Shannon. The one in the photo.

'Hi, Tommo. Hi, Georgie,' she says.

'Hi, Shannon,' says Tommo. 'Where are you off to this morning?'

'Heading into town,' says Shannon. 'Do a bit of shopping.'

'Good one,' says Tommo. 'Georgie and I are just going out for a while, too. Catch the sun while it's out.'

'Have fun,' she says.

And then, while Tommo goes to unlock the door, she turns to look at me. 'You all right, Georgie?' she says.

My eyes slip away. I don't really look at people, not properly.

But then they slide back to her, for some reason, and she's still there, still smiling. Big, open, sunny smile, like in the pictures that keep appearing under my door. A look of concern, too, behind the smile. The look of someone who means it. Someone who cares.

I'm watching her face, her eyes, and she doesn't look away. I realise it's a real question and she's waiting, expecting an answer.

My mouth falls open. Then closes again.

Shannon, I think, as we walk down the drive. Shannon.

'Just take it one step at a time,' says Tommo. He doesn't rush me. Doesn't try to hold my hand, either. Isn't that dangerous? Mightn't I do something silly? Mightn't I run off?

It's lovely. The yellow flowers are out, all down the lane. Daffodils, Tommo says. The sun's out, too. It's a long time since I've felt the warmth of the sun on my face.

At the bottom there's a bench. We sit down and

rest. I have to narrow my eyes to stop the sun dazzling me. They're not used to the brightness any more. We sit in silence, at ease with one another, sort of, and then Tommo starts talking.

'It reminds me of the summer I worked in a laundry, this,' he says. 'The summer I left college. I had to get up at six every morning and cycle into town. It was always my favourite part of the day, that, riding through the early morning mist, along the river all lined with daffodils. I'd get to the laundry, start up the van and trundle down to the station. Up on the platform, where the overnight bags had been unloaded off the trains. All the laundry from all the trains, all over the country. One by one I hauled them into the van and when I'd done all that I drove back to the laundry. I dragged the bags out of the back of the van and spent the rest of the day pulling out the contents and sorting them into separate piles, ready for washing. Sheets in one pile, towels in another, pillowcases in a third. That's what I did all day long – sat under this tower of dirty laundry, sorting. Sheets, towels and pillowcases. Sheets, towels and pillowcases.'

He goes quiet again, lost in thought.

'You wouldn't believe how many there were,' he goes on. 'Sometimes I'd look up at the great pile of laundry bags towering above me and I'd start to panic. I'll never get it done, I'd say. There'll be a whole load left at the end of the day and then there'll be nowhere to put tomorrow's. The railways will run out of clean laundry and people travelling from one end of the country to another will have to sit up all night. They won't be able to work the next day, because they haven't had enough sleep. And all because I'm too slow.'

I'm not sure why he's telling me all this, sitting on the bench, staring into the distance, remembering. But the words are painting pictures in my mind, and I'm there, in the laundry, beside him.

'So I'd start to hurry,' he says. 'I'd work faster and faster, till I was out of breath. Sheet, towel, pillowcase, sheet, towel, pillowcase, sheet, pillowcase, towel. I'd start putting them in the wrong piles and I'd have to get up and sort it out. And every time I looked up there'd seem to be just as much left to sort as before. I'd panic, throwing things all over the place, making even more mistakes. In the end I'd have to stop, and still the great pile of laundry would loom above me.'

I can see them, feel them, all around me. Pressing in on me. Hemming me in. Sheets, towels and pillowcases. Sheets, towels and pillowcases.

'It was starting to get me down,' he says, 'until Andy came back from holiday and told me that wasn't the way to do it all. "Keep cool, man," he said. "Take it one step at a time. Don't think of the whole pile all at once. Just concentrate on the next bag, and the next. The next towel, the next sheet, the next pillowcase. Make up stories in your head about the people who used them. The family going on holiday, the politician on his way to an important meeting, the friends off to a show . . . Don't try to do it all at once, or it becomes too much for you. Because the faster you work, the longer it takes, that's what I find. You mess up, and it's not worth the hassle. Go slowly, carefully. When you're tired, stop and rest. And all at once, before you know it, the pile's gone. Your day's work's over. No problem."'

Tommo stands up.

'So that's what I did,' he says, turning to me and smiling. 'And it worked.'

And then we walk, one step at a time, back to school.

shannon

I was right about Tommo coming in. He was here first thing. I was in the kitchen, helping to wash up after breakfast, and he came in to get a cup of coffee.

'How's it going with Georgie?' I asked him.

'Oh, not so bad,' he said, with a gleam in his eye. 'I might even get him outside, if I'm lucky.'

'So is he talking yet?' I said.

'Give us a chance, Shannon,' said Tommo, with a smile. 'He's only just arrived.'

We were all set to go off into town, me and the others, but I did one of my disappearing acts. I knew they wouldn't go without me. I hung round for a while, hoping I might spot him. Georgie, I mean. I'm dead nosy like that. I just wanted to see him close up, to see how he was.

Next thing they're coming down the stairs together, him and Tommo. That guy's amazing –

no one else could have done it so quick. Anyway, I waited till they were almost down, came out from my hiding place and strolled across the hallway, as if I'd just met them by chance.

'Hi, Tommo. Hi, Georgie,' I said, grinning up at them.

I was going to have a bit of a chat with Tommo, but he was flashing me a warning look. Don't mess it up, he was saying. Don't blow it. Then he went over to open the door, leaving me and Georgie alone for a second.

'How's it going, Georgie?' I said, giving it all I'd got. Smiley face, twinkly eyes. 'All right?'

He looked away, all shy like. But then he glanced back, into my eyes, and opened his mouth.

'Yeah,' he said, nodding his head. It wasn't more than a whisper, but he said it all right! I know he did!

I went into town then. Did all the usual stuff, hanging round the record store, buying fags, smoking with the townie lads down by the bus station, but my heart wasn't in it. For the first time ever I didn't really want to be there. I wanted to be back here in school.

Because all the time I was there I was thinking of Georgie. I'd done it! I'd got him to talk!

6 april

I wake, look around and remember. Remember where I am, what I did yesterday. I find the photo of Shannon and smile. I like her. She's the sort of person I could be. One day.

There's another smiley face under the door. This time it's different. It's made up of pictures cut out of a magazine. There's a face, a cartoon face, and underneath it there's the wavy lines, and this time I know what they are. A river, a beautiful river.

The face makes me laugh. It's some sort of dog, I think, a cartoon dog.

The river's a whole different mood. It's cool, strong. It makes me feel cool and strong just to look at it.

That's how I'd like to be, you know. Part dog, part river. Happy, cool, strong. That's the new Georgie. That's how I'm going to be. One day.

I look at the page one more time and put it

under my pillow with the rest. And as I'm doing so, I make up my mind. Today's the day, Georgie. Today's the first day of the rest of your life.

I climb out of bed, pull on some clothes and go and wait outside my room. I'm going to try it. Try and go downstairs. Am I ready? Will I ever be ready? If I wait till I've a long grey beard and a hibbly-hobbly walking stick, will I be ready? Probably not. So now's as good a time as any.

Go for it, Georgie! Make a fresh start. Take the chance to be normal.

'Hello, Georgie,' says the fair-haired woman, carrying some clothes. 'Nice to see you up and about. Do you want me to bring up your breakfast?'

I shake my head no.

She looks at me more closely. 'Do you want to come down and have it with the others?' she asks, trying to hide her surprise.

I nod yes.

'That's great!' she says breezily. 'Hang on a sec and I'll be right with you. I've just got to give these to Alan.'

She goes into the room across the corridor and I

see her handing the clothes to the boy.

She comes back over and I hold out my hand. She leads me to the top of the stairs and off we go. Halfway down I notice the beautiful coloured window. It's tall and thin and the sunlight streams through it in reds and blues and greens. It must have been there when I came up the first time, but I was in such a state that I didn't even notice it.

'Stained glass,' she says, smiling. 'It's lovely, isn't it?'

But Alan, fully dressed now, rushes past, flying down the stairs three at a time. He pushes me out of the way and I have to grab the banister to stop myself from falling.

'Alan!' the woman cries. 'Watch where you're going! Come back here and say sorry to Georgie!'

But Alan's gone.

'Oh, dear,' says the woman. 'He's always in a hurry, that one, especially at mealtimes. Likes his food, does our Alan. He doesn't mean any harm, though.'

I sit on the stair and breathe. Slowly, deeply. Seconds pass, minutes pass and I'm still there. Everyone else goes past me, around me. The staff say, 'Morning, Georgie,' and go on. The boys either rush down without even noticing me, or stop and stare. No sign of Shannon. I suppose the girls are somewhere else.

When it's all quiet again, I get up and walk slowly back to my bedroom. The woman comes with me, stays with me.

'Never mind, Georgie,' she says. 'The important thing is that you tried. Maybe next time.'

Then she goes down and fetches my breakfast.

later

Hannah, that's her name. She tells me when she comes back up to take the tray away. She stays for a while and I show her my bird book.

I like her. I like nearly everyone here. They're different.

She comes back later and asks me if I want to come down for lunch. I'm not sure, after what happened this morning, but she tells me that everyone else is outside at the moment, so there's no chance of anyone pushing past me on the stairs.

I remember Tommo's story about the laundry. If I keep trying, it's OK. If I get a bit further each time, it's OK. I don't need to be mad at myself or at anyone else if it doesn't work out. As long as I keep trying.

I remember Shannon's cheeky grin, too. She wouldn't let someone like Alan stop her, now would she? If she decided to do something, she'd just go ahead and do it.

So down we go, taking it slowly, one step at a time. Past the stained-glass window, stopping, but only briefly, to breathe in its calmness, its beauty. Then down the second flight of stairs, across the hall and into the houseroom, my houseroom.

Hannah leads me across to the far side and we sit on the large, squashy sofa together. It's quiet, a big room with a high ceiling, all yellow. I can hear music playing, gentle music.

I can see the others outside in the play area. There's Alan, over by the swings, and Shannon, sitting on a bench with her Walkman on, reading a magazine.

'They'll be coming in for their lunch in a few minutes,' Hannah tells me. 'I thought we'd just come down a bit early so you'd have a chance to get used to the room. When the others come in, see how you feel. If you want to sit at the table and eat with them, that's fine. If you'd rather eat off a tray, here on the sofa, that's fine too. And if you'd like to go back upstairs, there's no problem. OK?'

I nod OK. I'm watching Shannon through the window. Every time my eyes wander around the yard, looking at the other children, they slip back to her for comfort. It's busy outside – too busy for me. Too many people I don't know, too much going on. But watching Shannon makes me feel calm.

They're big, especially the boys. Very different from the kids at the Birches. I'm watching one of them, and I can tell he's looking at Shannon. Suddenly he runs over to the bench and tries to grab her magazine. Shannon won't let go.

The boy pulls, Shannon pulls and the pages rip. The boy falls over, Shannon cries out, and suddenly she pulls back her foot and thumps it into his side. He gets up, lunges at her, grabs a handful of her hair and tugs. Her Walkman goes flying across the yard as she screams.

A man runs over, but the boy lashes out at him too. He's kicking and punching, and he won't let go of Shannon's hair. She's kicking and punching too, and in the end it takes three staff to get them apart. They march the boy across the yard and he's still fighting, still yelling. All the other children move away from him.

He's coming this way. Surely they won't bring him in here. Surely they've got more sense. I tense up. My knees are shaking.

Hannah jumps up from the sofa, hurries over to the glass door and waves them away. 'No,' she says. 'Don't bring him in here.' But they ignore her. The boy's too wild, too dangerous, and they have to get him off the yard before he does any more damage. One of the staff unlocks the door and in he comes, into the room. My room.

I run to the other door, the one that leads to the stairs. Hannah comes after me and tries to bustle me out so I don't see. But I want to see, I have to see. I'm outside the room now, but I stay by the door, holding it slightly open, peeping round. I'm ready to run if the boy comes my way, but I watch, fascinated.

They've got him sitting in the middle of the sofa. There's a member of staff on each side, holding his arms to stop them swinging so wildly. Another man's kneeling on the floor holding his legs to stop him kicking. They've taken his shoes off so he can't do so much damage. Bob, they call him. 'Cool it, Bob.'

He's screaming and yelling and shaking his head from side to side. They're not hurting him, I can tell. They're not holding him too tightly, like Keith does. They're only trying to protect him from himself, to stop him from damaging anyone, but still it's horrible to watch.

A young woman's clinging to one of his arms, terrified. You can see just by looking at her that it's her first time. She's holding him as best she can but she's not strong enough, not confident enough. The boy's wild, completely wild. Fighting to throw them off him, he's pulling one way, pulling another, testing each one of them to the limit.

Suddenly Bob goes quiet. I watch the woman's face. She's shocked, exhausted, and she thinks that now he's quiet it's over, she thinks the fight's gone out of him. She relaxes her grip for a split second, and, sensing it, he jerks away from her, freeing himself from her grasp. She realises her mistake and tries to grab hold of his arm again but he's too quick for her. As her hand bounces off his arm and slips past his face, he sinks his teeth into her wrist and she screams.

All this time I'm standing by the door, spell-bound. I've seen it all before and yet I've never seen it, not from the outside, not as clearly as this. It's as though I'm looking in a mirror, but there's no mirror. I know he's called Bob, this boy, but he might as well be me, Georgie Bayliss. Because that's how I've been, many, many times. Worse too, much worse.

later

I try to eat my lunch alone in my room, but I feel sick. Sick to my stomach because I've failed, yet again. Why is it so hard? All I'm trying to do is go downstairs and eat with other people. It's not such a big deal, is it? But every time I try there's always someone or something getting in my way, someone or something stopping me.

I'm thinking about Tommo, and how he said it takes time. I know he's right, but I so wanted to please him. I wanted him to come in tomorrow and hear that I went to the houseroom and sat at the table with all the others. He'd have been so pleased. He'd have come bursting into my room and said, 'Well done, Georgie!' He might even have tried to hug me. And now he won't. Because of Bob. No, because of me.

I'm thinking about Shannon, too. Shannon and her temper. I hope she's OK.

She's like me, really. I hadn't seen that before. Further down the line, of course, but I've this sneaky feeling that in a whole lot of ways she's just like me.

In a way I'm disappointed that she was quite so angry, quite so violent, because I wanted her to be perfect. I sort of wanted her to be something special, something different. But in another way I'm not disappointed. Because it means she's human. Like me.

So I'm glad she's got a temper, really. Because it's good to know that you can be OK, like Shannon, and still lose control sometimes. Maybe, just maybe, I haven't got as far to go as I thought.

Mind you, I'd have gone wild if Bob had gone for me like that. And if he busted my Walkman, if I ever had a Walkman, I'd kill him.

And suddenly there's Tommo at the door. It's Sunday, but he's come in anyway. Come in to see me again.

'Hi, Georgie,' he says. 'How about another walk?'

I'm so pleased to see him I don't have time to say no, even if I wanted to. I nod yes, and follow him down the stairs. He opens the big wooden door and out we go, down the lane.

When we get to the bench where he told me about the laundry, about taking it one step at a time, we don't stop. He opens the gates; we cross the road and climb a stile into a field. There are sheep in the field. Sheep and lambs.

Some of the lambs are lying on the grass, soaking up the sunshine. I watch one mother, worried because we're coming close, go over to protect her little one from these invaders, these humans. The lamb gets up on its wobbly legs, takes one look at us and turns away to nuzzle into her.

A group of lambs, slightly bigger than the others, are playing on a grassy hump. As I watch them, I realise that I know what they're playing. I played it myself in another life. When I was the king of the castle.

Some of the sheep call their lambs, but they're too busy bouncing to notice. We come quite close to them before they see us. Then one looks up and alerts the others. They panic and run in every direction, back to their mothers. Most find them straight away but one little black one can't and bleats, frightened. She sees us coming ever closer, and she freezes. A sheep looks up from the other side of the field and answers her call.

The lamb watches us with tiny, terrified eyes. She knows where her mother is, but she doesn't know how to get there. She wants to run in a straight line, the only way she knows, but she can't, because we're in the way. The mother sheep is calling but isn't able to come over because her other lamb's beside her, feeding. It's up to the tiny black lamb to reach her mother.

I'm watching, unable to move. I know what it's like to be that lamb, stranded, alone. And yet I'm the reason it can't get to its mother. Then I notice that Tommo, ahead of me, has changed direction, skirting round the lamb so as not to worry her. I follow him, and when the lamb sees that the coast is clear, she dashes to her mother. Once she gets there, she pushes the second lamb out of the way and butts in, gulping down great mouthfuls of milk. I smile.

Tommo leads me through a gate into another field, and we follow a path that runs along a fence, all the way up the hill. I'm out of breath long before we get to the top, but I pull myself from fencepost to fencepost and somehow I manage to keep going. Whenever I fall too far behind, Tommo stops and waits for me.

We sit side by side on a rock. Tommo pulls out a

bottle of water and shares it with me. He digs deep into his pocket, hands me a Mars bar, and on we go.

He's whistling a tune, a happy tune that rises and falls as we walk, that goes up and down and around for ever. It's the music inside him, the joy of being in the mountains.

He doesn't say much, Tommo. He doesn't have to. It's all right not to talk when you're walking up a hill. It doesn't mean there's anything wrong with you. It's all right not to speak to the person next to you. It doesn't mean you don't like them. Silence is good, walking up a hill. Silence or whistling. They both mean you're happy. They mean you're at peace. At peace with yourself. At peace with the mountain.

When we get to the top the view is amazing. You can see for miles in every direction. The sea on one side, the mountains all around. And the sky – I never knew there was so much sky. I lie back and let the clouds lift me up, up and away.

The school's tiny, and I can see a town in the distance – the town Shannon was off to yesterday, most likely.

'Yeah, that's where she went,' says Tommo,

reading my mind. 'All hustle and bustle down there. I'd rather be up here on a day like this, wouldn't you, Georgie?'

I nod. I would. I really would.

later

This time I'm going to do it. For Tommo. For Shannon. This time I'm going to do it for me.

I go out of my room. There's no one about. I cross the landing and start off down the stairs. I stop by the window, the stained-glass window. I let the colours stream into my head, fill my body. To warm me up, to give me strength, to keep the whiteness of my fear and anger at bay.

Then I carry on down the stairs, slowly, steadily. A door opens below me and I freeze. A boy comes flying out of one room, dashes across the hall and in through another door. It's Alan, the one who nearly pushed me down the stairs. He doesn't see me.

I get to the bottom. I cross over to the house-room door and put my ear up against it. All I can hear is music, quiet music. Maybe there's no one in.

I open the door a crack and peep through. There're lots of people inside, and I catch my breath, shocked. I look at the sofa, the one I was sitting on earlier. Luckily there's no one there, so I make my way over and sit down, breathing slowly, deeply, staying in control. Just. Everyone looks up as I cross the room, but I pretend not to notice.

The adults all carry on with what they're doing, keeping it cool, acting as though there's nothing special going on. But one of the boys at the table pushes back his chair and rushes over. I look round at the staff, to see if they're going to do anything. I can see alarm on their faces, but they don't move. Not yet. They're going to wait, wait to see what happens.

The boy pushes up next to me, squeezing me into the arm of the chair, and I don't like it. He's squeaking with excitement, dribbling all down himself, all over me. Hannah realises it's time to come to the rescue and hurries across, sitting down on the other side of him.

'Hello, Georgie,' she says, leaning across him, smiling. 'It's nice to see you. Have you come down for tea?'

I'm about to nod yes, but the boy starts pulling at my jumper and I don't like it. I don't like it at all.

'Don't do that, please, Mark,' says Hannah, and she takes his hands away. But then he puts his dribbly face up close to mine. Too close. As though he's about to kiss me.

'He's just curious,' says Hannah, pulling him back. 'He's never seen you before.'

I know. I can tell he doesn't mean any harm, but I still don't like it.

'Do you want to come outside and play football, Mark?' says a man, going over to the door to the yard and unlocking it. It's the right thing to say, because Mark jumps up and follows him out. My breathing settles.

Hannah smiles, moves a bit closer to me and we're quiet. For a long time, we're quiet. I look round the room at all the faces. None of them are watching me any more. They're just getting on with what they were doing before I came in. And it feels safe. Safe enough, anyway.

There's nothing I want to do, not till mealtime. I hope it's soon. Not because I'm hungry, just because I want to – have to – get this over with. I wonder where Shannon is, what she's doing. I thought maybe she'd be here, but she's not. So I sit back. Listen to the music. Sit very still, very quiet so no one notices me, no one bothers me.

After what seems like ages the door swings open and I see a member of staff wheeling in a trolley with some food on it. Suddenly the room comes alive. The table's cleared and set for tea, and everyone goes over and sits down. The man and the boy come in from outside. Someone goes to fetch Alan from the other houseroom.

'Would you like to join us, Georgie?' asks Hannah, and I find myself nodding. I put out my hand and she helps me up, out of the sofa and over to the table. Slowly, carefully.

'This is your chair,' she says. I look at it closely and then sit down. Hannah puts my food in front of me, while the others serve themselves, sort of.

It's spaghetti. Messy food. But I haven't time to think about being tidy, staying clean. It's hard enough sitting here, with everyone so close I can taste their breath. It's hard enough without worrying about how I look.

So I eat it quickly. Shovel it into my mouth so fast that the sauce splatters all down my front. I swallow it down with great mouthfuls of water. I don't bother about the mess I'm making. I don't bother about Alan, who's sitting across from me, burrowing into his food like he hasn't eaten for months. Or about Mark, who's watching me the whole time, much more interested in me than his food.

I don't care what they think of me, all those staff, oh so carefully not watching, oh so carefully getting on with what they're doing. The point is to close my mind to everything else and just do it. For the first time in ages to eat a meal with other people, like any normal human being does every single day of their lives. That's not so much to ask, is it?

So I don't look at anyone else, don't think about anything else. I finish my meal, push back my chair and run. Out the door, up the stairs and into my bedroom.

Yes!

I did it!

I beam at the old Georgie, stuck in the mirror, stuck in this room, stuck on his own in the past. I stick out my tongue at him, pull down my pants and flash my bum at his mucky face, all splattered with sauce.

Then I switch on my stereo and blast out the room. I dance and I dance till my stomach cramps from eating so fast and I have to lie on my bed and steady my breathing.

But who cares? I did it!

shannon

I really blew it today. I'd been edgy all morning, full of aches and pains, trying to keep it together and just about hanging on in there. Staying apart, keeping myself to myself. Just before lunch I was sitting on the bench outside, hiding behind my favourite band and my favourite magazine, when that stupid tosser Bob went and threw a wobbly. Came flying across the yard like his arse was on fire, and tried to grab my magazine.

No way I was going to let him have it, of course. Why should I? I mean, he can't even read, for God's sake. 'Sod off!' I said, and he pulled even harder. Next thing I knew it's ripped down the middle, my Walkman flies off my head, Bob hits the floor and I'm putting the boot in. Big time.

He reached up then and grabbed a handful of my hair. God, it hurt! I yelled, everyone ran over to drag him off me and I was left there on the bench, tears streaming down my face.

And then I saw Georgie. He was in the house-room, and he'd seen the whole thing! And now he was standing by the door, watching Bob coming towards him, terrified.

He saw me. Saw me for the bitch I am. Typical. Just bloody typical. First time I lose it in weeks, and he's there, watching.

Why do I have to act like that? I mean, what am I trying to prove? I wish I could grow up, you know. I wish I could learn to act my bleeding age.

I so wanted to help Georgie. I so wanted him to like me, to think I was normal. The smiley, happy Shannon. But I'm not. I'm just like all the rest. Problem kids. More trouble than we're worth.

A danger to society, that's what they say. Lock us up and throw away the key. Dump us in a school in Wales, miles from anywhere, and forget about us, that's what they say.

Maybe they're right. Maybe they're right.

What'll Georgie think of me now?

into memory

It's Monday morning. I know because Sally came up to see me earlier and told me. I'd just put my new smiley man under my pillow. Who's sending them? Sally? Tommo? Hannah? One of the kids?

What are they telling me – look on the bright side? Grin and bear it?

Sally said Tommo would pop in first thing. He wouldn't be able to spend much time with me, though, because he'd have to be over in school, teaching. Unless I wanted to go with him, that is.

There's a knock on the door and it's him. 'Hey, I heard about yesterday evening, Georgie,' he says, beaming. 'Well done! I think you're brilliant!'

He comes over to hug me, sitting up in bed, and I don't mind. In fact, instead of hanging limp like they usually do, my arms almost come together behind his back. I don't exactly hug him, but it's a start.

I'm really pleased with myself, and shocked too. Too shocked to notice what I'm doing, what I'm saying, even.

Tommo walks across the room and stands by the window.

'Can you talk, Georgie?' he says.

'Yeah.' The word slips out without my thinking. His question takes me so much by surprise that I forget who I am, forget how I'm supposed to be.

Why? Why did I say it? How did I say it? It's because I spoke to Shannon the other day, isn't it? Did I speak to Shannon?

He turns towards me, blinks hard. 'So what can you say?'

'Yeah . . . no . . . ' The words are bubbling up now, up from somewhere lost, and I can't seem to stop them.

They sound strange, so strange after all this time. My voice is different, deeper. Sort of hoarse, husky. Loud, too, though I know I'm only whispering.

'Georgie . . . Mummy . . . '

Mummy. Oh, God, why did I say that? Of all the words I could have said, why was it that one?

'Where's Mummy, Georgie?'

Don't know. I don't know.

I go all rigid, pull up my knees, drop my head, wrap my arms tightly, tightly around myself. To stop the words, stop the thoughts. To stop the feeling, the breathing. I shut myself down, hold my breath, to stop the moment, to stop the world from turning.

And Tommo sees. Tommo knows. He watches me stiffen but he doesn't back away. He sees the fear, the fear that comes before anger. He knows we're in danger, both of us, but he doesn't run, doesn't try to escape. Others would, but not him. Not Tommo.

'She's gone, love,' he says, easing his words into the silence before it has a chance to take control. 'She can't come back, ever. You know that, don't you?'

I raise my head. Slowly, ever so slowly. I raise my head and our eyes meet.

'I'm sorry, Georgie,' he says. 'I'm so sorry. But your mummy's dead.'

I stare at him. Stare at him for ever. I'm hearing

him but I'm not hearing him. It's as though he's using a different language or something.

His lips are moving. There are sounds coming out, but there's a thick fog in the room. A thick fog that stops them getting through to my brain.

He says it again, coming closer. 'She's dead, love. Surely they told you?'

I'm hearing the words more clearly now, but I still can't quite grasp their meaning. I hear them, and I can tell from his face, from the thickness of the fog that surrounds them, that it's important. Important to try and understand.

His eyes are holding mine. His clear, blue, piercing eyes. They don't waver. They're never going to waver.

It's up to me to look away. It's up to me to hide. I have a choice. I can let the fog swallow me. I can crawl back into my shell, where it's safe. Or I can listen, concentrate, work out what he's trying to say, what it means for me.

I choose to listen. I force my brain to sift out all the rubbish that's getting in the way and to *listen*. And slowly, slowly his words begin to filter through the fog, filter into my brain.

Mummy.

Gone.

Mummy.

Dead.

I mouth the words back at him, soundlessly. I say them over and over in my head, trying to understand, trying to put them into some sort of context, give them some sort of meaning.

I know what the word 'Mummy' means. I know what the word 'gone' means. I think I know what the word 'dead' means. I know all these words, as words. But somehow I can't put them together. Together, in the same sentence, they don't seem to work, don't seem to make any sense.

I don't like them together. I don't understand them together. I've never heard them together, these words. I can't have, or I'd remember. Surely I'd remember.

Gone.

Dead.

Never coming back.

Tommo's close now. He's sitting on my bed next to

me. He's putting his arm around me and I'm sinking my head into his neck. The wool of his jumper. The softness of his hair. Sinking my head into the warmth of his skin.

I feel the tears coming, welling up from inside, from the very depths of me. I try to stop them, I desperately try to stop them, but I can't, I just can't.

So I cry. At last I cry.

I cry and Tommo doesn't leave me.

I cry and no one gets hurt.

I cry and my mind slips back seven years, to that awful, awful day.

I woke to silence. Not just the silence of early morning, a deeper, softer silence. I sat up in bed and saw a light, a rainbow of white streaming through the gap in the curtains, calling me.

I jumped out of bed and a shiver cut through me. Pulling on my dressing gown, I ran to the window, threw back the curtains and gasped. The world was white. Transformed.

'It's snowing!' I yelled, running from the room. 'Mum! It's snowing!'

Patch ran up the stairs to greet me, yelping at my

excitement. He leapt up into my arms, and together we ran into Mum's room and jumped on her bed. Mum grunted, pulling back the cover for me to slip in next to her.

Usually it was my favourite time, all snuggled up close, wrapped in her long, dark hair. We'd doze, we'd whisper, we'd share our dreams and leave it as long as possible to get out of bed. Or as long as Patch would let us, because he'd be whining and trying to pull the covers off the bed, begging for his breakfast, or to be let out into the garden.

But today there was no time to hang about. Winter had arrived and it was me, not Patch, begging to go outside.

'Can I build a snowman, Mum?' I cried. 'Can I stay off school?'

'I have to work this morning, love. There'd be no one to look after you.'

She felt me pull away. 'I'll tell you what,' she said. 'We'll build one now, together.'

No time to waste. We hopped out of the warm bed, threw on our clothes, scrabbled for our wellies in the cupboard under the stairs and ran out into the front garden, all giggling and laughing. Old Mrs Crabbyface next door twitched the curtain, wondering what all the fuss was about so early in the morning. I stuck out my tongue at her while Mum wasn't watching.

Mum got a spade and started shovelling all the snow into a big pile. I pressed it into a shape, two shapes, and in no time at all we'd made this great snowman. Big ball body, little ball head, two stones for his eyes, a carrot for his nose and an old woolly hat to keep his head warm.

'Aw, Mum, I can't leave him here on his own all day,' I said, tossing a snowball at her. 'Please let me stay.'

'Sorry, love,' she said, laughing and throwing one back at me. 'He'll probably still be here when you get home, though. If it stays as cold as this, I'm sure he won't melt.'

We went inside and I warmed myself by the radiator while Mum cooked up some porridge. Steaming hot.

'Eat up now or you'll be late for the bus,' she said, plonking it down in front of me. 'And I'll be late for work.'

I grabbed my bag and I was gone, skidding along the footpath, making snowball after snowball till my hands were raw. Chucking them at cars and bikes, dogs and cats, anything that moved and most things that didn't.

Mum was right, I was late for the bus. But the bus was late for me, too, so that was all right.

I open my eyes wide. I want to stop there. Stop at the good bit, the happy bit. Because it's about to change. Everything's about to change.

I'm afraid. Afraid of what comes next. So I force myself back into the present, the here and now. My room. Abernant. Tommo close beside me.

I look into his eyes, his clear, blue eyes, and I can tell that he knows. Knows where I am, where I'm going. And that he wants me, expects me, to carry on. Deeper, further, into the truth.

I shiver, and he holds me. The tears return, and he doesn't leave me. He doesn't ask any questions. There's no need. He just holds me, holds me as I cry, holds me as I remember.

I'm scared, so scared of where it's taking me. But I'm going to let it take me. It's time.

memory 2

School was over and I was on my way home. There was a rip in the knee of my new trousers from crashing to the ground on the ice slide we'd made in the school yard. A bruise above my left eye from the snowball Dougie Ryan thumped me with – I'm sure he'd put a stone in it.

So there I was, ripped, bruised and happy. I couldn't wait to get back and see if my snowman was still in the garden. The sky was turning dark again and it didn't feel any warmer, didn't feel as though it could have melted, but I had to see it. I had to be sure.

I couldn't wait to see Mum, either, even if she was going to tell me off about the trousers. But I knew she wouldn't be cross for long – she never was.

She only worked in the mornings, so she'd be there in the kitchen, waiting for me with a cup of tea and a plate of scones, hot buttered scones. I'd wait till she'd calmed down and then I'd ask her if she'd take me sledging up on Moulder Hill. All my friends were going.

The school bus pulled up on the corner. I grabbed my bag and ran along the aisle, punching Jim on the shoulder as I went past.

'I'll get you for that, Georgie Bayliss,' he said with a laugh.

I jumped down from the bus, into the slush of the gutter. It splattered all up my trousers, but I only laughed. Jim pressed his face up against the steamy window. It made his nose flat and his lips big. He stuck his tongue out.

I picked up a handful of snow, waited till the bus started to move and then I chucked it at him. It smacked against the glass right by his face, and I laughed again.

I ran up the road, skidding in the slush. I pushed open my gate and hurried up the path. I went over to my snowman, to see how much he'd melted. Hardly at all, just like Mum had said. He needed a bit of tidying up, though, and I was just about to start when Patch came scurrying out of the house, whining.

'What's wrong?' I said, looking up. 'What's wrong, silly?'

I don't know how I knew, but I knew. Something was wrong. Something terrible.

I ran to the front door and then I stopped. It was in there. Whatever it was, it was in there. I opened the door silently and crept in. Slowly, slowly, my feet slushing on the carpet. Afraid to go in. Afraid not to go in.

I heard a man's voice in the kitchen, a wild, angry voice. A voice I recognised. He was shouting something, over and over. I tried to work out what he was saying, but I couldn't.

I stood in the hall, frozen into stillness, into fear. Then I heard a scream, a horrible, horrible scream.

My eyes open wide again. Wide, to escape the memory of that awful moment. Wide, to bring me back into the present, into the warmth of Tommo's arms. And he holds me, holds me tightly. Holds me as I shake.

'You're doing well, Georgie,' he says. 'It's going to be OK.'

How can it be OK? How can it ever be OK?

Time passes. Everything's quiet. There's no one on the landing, no children running around, no Molly cleaners hoovering. Just Tommo, me and the silence.

At some point Sally's at the door. 'Don't worry, Tommo,' I hear her whisper. 'You stay with Georgie. I'll take over your class for today.'

And it's just us again. Me, Tommo and the silence. The silence I'm afraid to break, even by thought.

The day slips by, and the night, the next day and the one after.

I lie in bed, unable to think, unable to move. Ignoring the smiley men, all sorts of smiley men, every type of river flowing under my door. Happiness and strength, joy and calmness, laughter and power, if I could only bring myself to crawl out of bed and accept them.

There are people out there who care about me, the messages say. People who'd like to help me find out what sort of a person I really am, who'd like to help me live as I'm supposed to live. People out there who could like me, maybe even love me, if I come through this.

I have to start by accepting what happened. I know that. But how am I to face living with it? How am I to face a future of remembering?

I can't. I lie in bed, unable to open wider the

door into the future. Because somehow it's the same door. The door to the past is the door to the future. The door to the future is the door to the past. The door that brings the river, the door that brings the smiles, is the very same door that brings the nightmares, the blood, the screaming. Open that door and everything changes. Open that door, Georgie boy, and all your protection slips away, all the thick, scaly skin that you've built up over these years to stop the pain, it all slips off you and you're as vulnerable as the day you were born. And who'll take care of you then? Your mother? Your *mother*?

I lie there for days. For weeks. Sleeping, waking, fevered, remembering. As much as I'm trying to block it out, I'm remembering.

Only waking when Tommo's there. Only remembering when Tommo's there, because it's too painful otherwise.

Reaching that scream. Always reaching that scream. Wanting to scream myself. But I can't.

memory 3

Slowly, gradually, more and more each day. Letting it in, pushing it away, letting in a bit more, pushing it away, slowly, slowly, remembering . . .

It was Mum. I knew it was Mum but I didn't understand. I didn't understand what was happening. I struggled to break free from the ice that was freezing me to the floor. I ran towards her, to help her, but when I got to the kitchen doorway I turned to ice again. Frozen solid.

She was there and yet she wasn't there. She was lying on the floor and there was a man kneeling over her with a knife in his hand. Everything was red, all red, and his head began to turn, to look at me.

I couldn't bear it. Couldn't bear to see who it was. Couldn't bear to think what was happening, what might happen.

I ran. Out the door, into the icy street. I had to escape,

I had to get help, I had to run. Down the road, slipping, sliding. Patch at my heels, barking madly.

I forced the redness from my mind, and all the colours of the world went with it, draining away, leaving only whiteness.

I was running across the road. Running too fast. My bag fell from my shoulder. Books spilled out all over the road.

The roar of a car horn. The squealing of brakes. I opened my mouth to scream, but nothing came out.

Not a sound.

Not ever.

'It's all right,' says Tommo, holding me. 'It's all right.'

But it's not all right. It's all wrong. It's always been wrong. It doesn't make any sense. None if it makes any sense.

I cry then. I cry for what seems like hours, beating my fists on Tommo's shoulders until all my strength is gone. Great, heaving, breathless, throat-hurting gulps. Rivers of tears pouring from my eyes until I'm bone dry inside.

It's dark. I've been sleeping. A giant sob wakes me and I sit up, look around. There's a shape by the window. A quiet humming.

'It's OK, Georgie,' says Tommo, turning. 'It's just me.'

I lie back down again. Whimper, and sleep.

It's light. Tommo's still there, in the chair by the window. I watch him sleeping. I hear him snoring.

He stayed all day and all night. For me.

I close my eyes again, slip away again.

'I have to go over to school,' says Tommo, waking me gently. 'But I'll pop back later. Hannah will sit with you for now. Is that all right?'

I nod my head. I reach out and touch his hand.

I wake, and there's someone at the door. Hannah goes over and takes the tray from them.

'Here's some food, Georgie,' she says in her gentle voice. 'Do you want to eat?'

I don't know. She puts the tray on the table by my bed. I lean over and drink something, eat something. I don't know what it is. I'm too tired to even think about it. I've never been so tired in my whole life.

I wake, and Hannah's in the chair by the window, watching, waiting.

You can go, I whisper. I'll be OK on my own now. I don't whisper it out loud, but somehow she knows what I mean.

Hannah smiles. She comes over and kisses me on the cheek. Her lips are soft. She smells of flowers. She leaves me to the silence, leaves me to sleep.

I sleep.

I wake.

It's dark.

It's light.

Tommo's there.

Hannah's there.

No one's there.

Food's there.

Drink's there.

Nothing's there.

And my watch is by my pillow, ticking, ticking. Hours, days, it doesn't matter.

'Take your time, Georgie,' says Tommo. 'Take your time.'

14 may

There's a woman leaning over me, kissing me. Her hair, her long, dark, beautiful hair is brushing my face. Her warm lips touch my forehead. I breathe in her smell, the smell of flowers, the smell of morning.

I reach out to touch her, to caress her skin, to wrap myself in her hair. I reach out to touch her and she's gone. I close my eyes tightly, desperate to recapture her, but she's slipped away, back into my dreams, my memory.

I open them again, look all around, and there's no one there. Only a man, rising from the chair by the window. Tommo.

'Morning, Georgie,' he says. 'I didn't want to wake you, you were sleeping so deeply. But I have to go now, I'm afraid. It's twenty to ten – they'll be needing me in class.'

I can't focus on his words. They're not what I

want to hear. It's not his voice that I want to hear. Who was it? Who was it, there beside me? Say it, Georgie. *Say it!*

Mummy. It was Mummy. She came to wake me, to draw me into the day. She brought me a memory, a memory of when everything was good. She's gone now, but maybe she came for a reason.

I look over at Tommo, and there's something strange about him, a shiny brightness coming out of him. I sit up, blink a few times, and I see that it's not just Tommo, it's all around. The brightness is all around, and everything's clearer, more real.

I shut my eyes to cut out the dazzle, only to find that it's still there. The light's still shining inside my head.

I open my eyes and I can see. See clearly. There's a sharper, cleaner feel to the world, and it's amazing.

I close them again, to stop, to work out what's going on, and I find that I can think, too. All the lights are coming on inside my brain. Slowly, one by one, they're shining on my thoughts, connecting up the pathways, making things work.

It's like there's been a mist, a fog, over everything, and at last it's starting to clear. Like there's been a cloud hovering above me, pressing down on me. Not letting me move forward. Not letting me grow. Not letting me be who I really am, never mind grow into the person I'm supposed to become. Not letting me connect – to anyone, anything, ever. For days and months and years the fog's been all around me, pressing me down, holding me back.

And now at last it's lifting, rising, floating off. Out, up and away. Out of my brain, up from my body, away beyond the sun, whose rays it was blocking, whose light it was hiding, whose laughter it stole.

I climb out of bed and stand by the window, next to Tommo's chair. I look out across the yard to the classrooms. Dazzled by the sunlight. By how clear everything is, inside my brain and out. By all the words that are floating around inside my head. Words I didn't even know I knew.

I look back into the darkness of the room, to rest my eyes, rest my brain. My eyes fall on Tommo, and I remember what it was he said. 'They'll be needing me in class,' he said.

And my hand is reaching out to him.

'You don't want me to go?' he asks, eyebrows raised.

I shake my head. No, that's not it. I don't think that's it.

He looks at me more closely. 'You want to come with me?' he suggests.

I hear his question and realise that it's the one my brain wants to ask. The first question about the future.

Maybe. Maybe I do. I look round my room again. It's a good room, a room to come back to. But I don't want to stay here on my own all day. Not with these thoughts, these memories that are all around me now. They crawled out of me, into this space, and they're lurking somewhere, under the bed, behind the mirror. Lurking in the hidden places, ready to jump back out at me when I'm on my own. Jump out at me in the shiny brightness that I'm now seeing, thinking. I couldn't cope with that. Not on my own. Not right now.

It's good they've come out. I know that. But if I

want to get on with my life, I don't want them around me all the time. I want to be able to put them behind me, put them away in a drawer marked DANGER. A drawer I can open when I choose to, and look at, think about. But a drawer I can close, lock up, a drawer only I have the key to.

There are questions I have to leave buried in that drawer. Questions I can't even bear to ask myself. Questions about who. About why.

'Don't think of it all at once,' Tommo said, 'or it becomes too much for you.'

He's right. For years I didn't think about it at all, about Mum, about what happened. I didn't think about it because I couldn't.

And now, because of Tommo and Shannon, because of this place, because of the smiling face that's been greeting me every morning, the flowing river that's been drawing me out of myself, because at last I'm ready to face it, to face the past, it's here, it's all around me. I've woken up from a dream, a nightmare, only to find it wasn't a dream at all. It's part of life, part of my life – it really happened.

I need to go over it many times to try to understand it. I'm not sure if I ever will understand it, because at the moment I don't see how it makes any sense, any sense at all, but I can't really get on with my life, my proper life, until I learn to live with it.

I know I've got to slow it down, to take it bit by bit, to stop for rests. I've got to keep busy, fill up my life with some of the day-to-day things normal people do. That way it won't have a chance to overpower me. I think.

And maybe, maybe in time, just like Tommo in the laundry, before I know it, it'll be done. Sorted. Gone.

So I'll leave them here for a while, those terrible memories, those unanswered questions, leave them here in the drawer marked DANGER to darken just a little bit before I look at them again. Maybe leave them here for that other Georgie to think about, the one in the mirror, the one whose eyes are still veiled.

Yes, I'll come back to them when I'm ready, when I've got more strength. But for now I'm going to lay them to rest, here, here in this room.

Because it's time for me to go out into the world.

To face the future.

I've been using all my energy, more energy that I ever really had, to keep it all down, keep it all secret, keep it hidden even from myself. And now that it's risen to the surface, now that I've had the courage, the help, to start to face it, I don't have to fight so hard. I've got some energy left over, maybe. To start living on the outside. To start to connect.

Tommo can read my mind. 'If you come over to school I could teach you numbers,' he says gently. 'So you can tell the time on your watch. Would you like that, Georgie?'

I would like that. That's one of the many things I'd like to do.

'I could help you learn to read,' he says.

I want that too. I want that more than almost anything.

'You can sit with Shannon. She's in my class too,' he says.

Do I want that? Can I bear to be in a classroom with other people? Tommo, yes, but other children? Other screwed-up children?

Shannon?

'Hey, these came when you were ill,' he says, picking up a pile of papers from beside my bed and handing them to me. 'One every morning, under your door.'

I take the papers. I look at them. Smiley, happy people, laughing and giggling. Cool, flowing rivers, raging torrents, calm waters. Drawings, paintings, photos, collages. Who gave me these? And why? What do they mean?

I know what they mean.

But why would someone go to so much trouble? Why would someone care?

I check under my pillow and the first ones are still there. I show them to Tommo. I point to a smile. And I smile. I point to the wavy lines. I raise my eyebrows in query.

'Shannon, I think,' Tommo answers with a laugh. 'It's the name of a river, in Ireland.'

And I nod. Shannon. Of course. The one with the magazine. The one with the twinkle in her eye. The one who said, 'See you later, Georgie.' Who looked into my eyes and settled me.

The one who lost her temper with Bob, too.

Who kicked and screamed and yelled.

She's the one who's been sending me messages. Every night. Or is it early morning? Creeping round the corridors while everyone's asleep. Sneaking past the night staff. For me.

So will I go with Tommo, over to school? Will I go and see Shannon, who's been working so hard for me? I want to say yes, but I'm frightened. I want to melt the ice, to stop the crying inside, but I'm scared, too. Scared of discovering who I really am. Scared of what I might find underneath.

I want to open up to myself, open up to other people, but I don't want to hurt them. I don't want them to hurt me. I want to turn my back on the old Georgie, on the years of sadness. But maybe he's part of me? Maybe I have to bring him with me.

I don't know. I don't know anything any more.

'Do you want to come?' Tommo asked me. And all I have to say is yes. One little word to change my life.

But this time I know it won't jump out by itself, like it did before, with Shannon. This time it won't just catch me by surprise, like a burp. This time I have to work at it, I have to mean it.

I search around inside. My head is filling up with words at last, words to describe, words to explain. But are they words for speaking, or only words for thinking? Words for me, or words to share? If I open my mouth to try and let them out, will they turn into sound? And if they turn into sound, will they be loud enough for anyone to hear? Will they make any sense? Is my voice too quiet for this noisy world? Too high? Too low? It's so long since I've spoken that I simply don't know.

But it's only one little word, one little three letter word, that I need. The easiest word there is, unless you're a Georgie, when no words are easy. Unless you're a sad, frightened little child, when the only thing you ever seem to say, if you say anything, is the other word, the no word.

But that's not me. I'm not going to let that be me. Not any more.

So I search around inside, in and out of the word banks of my mind, where I used to have a voice. Before it got stuck in my throat, before my breath was stolen from me, before I became speechless, dumb, mute. I search around in those long-disused places and I find it. Find the word I need.

I frame it with air from deep in my gut and I draw it up. Up through my lungs, up and up until it's nearly out. It's such a long way. Will I have the breath, the courage to bring it out into the world?

I open my mouth and it floats to the surface.

'Yes,' I say. Yes, I'll come.

And it's a real word. A sound word. I didn't bite it back. I didn't swallow it before it had a chance to find a voice. No, I can hear it with my own ears and so can Tommo. I can tell by the expression on his face.

I'm proud, so proud. I look at him and smile. A real smile, an open, happy smile.

And Tommo smiles back. He comes over and gives me a hug. There's a tear in the corner of his eye.

Then I pick up my watch and my bird book, and we head for the classroom.

shannon

Georgie came to school today! I was amazed to see him so soon. Tommo's been spending a lot of time with him lately, talking to him, making him safe. And I've been doing my bit, my Shannon bit. On the sly, like I do. Under the cover of darkness.

I knew we were making progress, me and Tommo, but I didn't realise quite how much. I didn't think for one minute that we'd get him over here yet, not for weeks.

Tommo brought him to my table and sat him down next to me.

'Morning, Shannon,' he said. 'Can Georgie sit here? Is that all right?'

He flashed me one of his looks. One of his take-it-easy looks. Maybe he doesn't know. Doesn't know how much this matters to me.

So I moved my books out of the way and made room for him. For Georgie, I mean. I didn't want to look him in the eye, though, because I was still ashamed.

I'd been so pleased when I got him to talk, so pleased that I'd done something good for once, something to help him. But then I'd gone and spoilt it all by scrapping with Bob just at the wrong time. Just when Georgie was watching.

Maybe I made up for it with my secret messages? Did he get them? Did he understand?

So I was avoiding Georgie's eye, in case he feared me, despised me. And he wasn't very happy either, of course. He was breathing funny, all shallow, panicky. First time he'd been to school in months, Tommo said.

His eyes were flitting round the room, looking for something to settle on. And then I felt them on me, and somehow I had no choice but to return his gaze. He found my eyes and I saw this deep calmness come over him.

He was looking into my head, into my soul. He saw my confusion, and he didn't mind. He'd seen me ranting, raging, and he understood. He saw my past, my history, and he shared it – somehow he shared it.

I looked straight back at him then. I saw some of his anger, his pain, his own dark history, and it was raw. He wanted to escape from it, to hide in me, and he was offering me a place to hide, too.

And then he smiled. A beautiful grin lit up his hollow face, transforming him. He was returning the gift. Thanking me for all those cold mornings when I'd climbed out of bed while everyone else was still asleep and sneaked down to the boys' end to deliver him a smile. A smile and a river, to give him hope.

Not that it was any great hardship. I always wake up round five. I don't seem to need much sleep. It's such a boring time of day, hanging round, waiting for everyone else to wake up. Listening to the silence, the birdsong, the squeaks, creaks and freaks of Abernant. Thinking, reading, or writing in my book.

The night staff don't like you having your light on, though. They come in, have a little chat to check you're OK, and then go out, switching it off after them.

So it's been good fun, getting one over on them.

Sneaking past their room, down the stairs, along the dark corridor, up the other stairs, shoving a message under Georgie's door, and back again without being seen.

Mind you, the other night I was nearly caught. I heard the radio on in the overnight room as I went past, so I thought Maggie was in there, knitting or darning socks or whatever turns you on, babe. But it turned out she was doing her rounds up the boys' end. I came round a corner and almost crashed into her! If I hadn't been right outside the boys' toilets she would have seen me for sure.

I nipped into a cubicle and pulled the door shut behind me, slipping the lock as quietly as I could. But she's got the ears of a bat, that one.

'Who's that?' she said, and I grunted, as deep as I could. I hoped she'd think it was one of the boys. They spend most of their time grunting, that lot.

I waited to hear her go, but she didn't. For fifteen minutes I was stuck in there, grunting and groaning and spinning the toilet roll to make it sound like I was for real. It must have been one of the longest fifteen minutes of my life. Why do boys have to be so disgusting? That place *stank*!

'Are you all right in there?' Maggie asked again. But she was getting bored by now, desperate to get back to her oh-so-thrilling knitting. I could tell by her tone of voice.

'Uuh,' I answered, as convincingly as possible. I waited another couple of minutes, imagining what she'd say if she found out it was me. Imagining what I'd say if one of the boys walked in!

Anyway, they didn't. And she didn't. I crept out, she'd gone, and I delivered a smile – a bit of a half-hearted smile by that time, I can tell you – under Georgie's door. Then I scarpered, fast.

Anyway, back to this morning. So there's Georgie, over in school for the first time ever, beaming at me, returning the smile. And as he did so, this weird feeling crept up from my toes, in from my fingers. It was some sort of a blush, I suppose. I've no idea why. I hate blushing, it's so embarrassing, but for once I didn't care who noticed. This was for me, me and Georgie, this moment. Nothing else mattered.

Me and Georgie. We know each other. We understand each other. Not completely, of course. I mean, I don't know what he's been through, what made him like this. He doesn't know what I've been through, either. Maybe I'll share some of it with him, some day, if we get close. Not all of it, though. I could never tell him all of it.

But I've got this strong feeling that he's going to be a friend, a real friend. Someone my own age who understands where I'm at, what it's like to be me. Someone my own age who's going through it too.

We'll hang on in there, me and Georgie. And maybe in time, maybe together, we'll both be OK.

29 may

Things are better. Much better.

I sleep with the curtains open so the sunlight wakes me in the morning. I sleep through the night, the demons from the past never find me, and I wake with a smile on my face, to the memory of my mother leaning over me, kissing me. Her long, dark hair brushing my face, her warm lips brushing my forehead.

I reach out to touch her, and she's gone. I close my eyes tightly, desperate to recapture her, her face, the way she looks, but she's gone, back into my dreams, my memory. And there's only her smell, the smell of flowers.

Yes, half-remembered faces, places, stay with me as I wake. But it's the good times that come back to me now, not the bad. Mummy, Ruby, the comfort of hair. Birthdays, Christmas, bathtime, holidays. A circus, a playground, the cinema, a zoo. The good times, remembered in my dreams.

They fade away with the birdsong and I turn on my music. I lie in bed for a while and then I get up. Check my post. I still get a message from Shannon every morning. But now it's in words, not pictures. Things that make me laugh – jokes and stuff. Followed by words that give me courage, the courage of a river. Not a lot of words, mind you, because I'm only new at this reading game, and some of them I don't understand. But they're words, real words. And they're for me.

You'd think someone would have caught her by now. A teenage girl running around the boys' corridor in the middle of the night! You'd think Tommo would have said something. There again, maybe not. Maybe it's his way of showing that he trusts us. That we're worthy of trust.

I go and have a wash before the morning rush. I come back and get dressed, and then I have a look at Georgie, the other Georgie, in the mirror. He looks OK. Not great, but OK. Dark lines under his eyes still. A gaunt, slightly haunted face. But so much better than he was. So much better.

And when I smile at him, these lines, these creases, sparkle from his eyes, circle his mouth and he looks almost human.

Poor old Georgie! I feel a bit guilty leaving him to sort out my problems, but it's such a relief to start putting them behind me. I've just got to get on with living.

'Keep an eye on things,' I whisper. 'Don't let it get to you.' And then I go down for breakfast. Down for breakfast! Hah!

It isn't easy. I still find some of the children here very strange. They make loud noises. They throw their food about the place. They're angry, some of them, very angry. Unpredictable, that's the worst thing. You just never know what it's going to be like. Sometimes everyone's as quiet as mice, eating, getting on with it. Other times they're crazy, every single one of them, and it's like feeding time at the zoo. Somebody starts, and it spreads like wildfire. At times like that, it's hard to remember that I'm the weirdest of the lot.

So, if things are really bad and it's starting to get to me, I take my food upstairs and eat it there. But I try not to, because it feels like I've failed when I do that, and I'm fed up with failing. I've been failing for more than half my life, and I'm done with it.

So most days I stay down with the others, in the houseroom. When I've finished my food, I go back up and wait for Tommo. I stand by the window, watching the sheep on the mountain, watching the colours change as the sunlight moves across the landscape.

Colour. There's so much colour here. Greens and blues and browns. I used to hate colour, because it always cheated me. It drained away whenever the anger took control. Or it took over my life, my brain. Red, the colour of blood. Brown, the colour of shit. That never happens now, none of it. I hold on to the colour, I hold on to myself, and I'm the one in control. I can't begin to explain how good that is.

I listen to my music. That's another thing I love. Another thing that's new in my life. I know all the songs, I hum along, and I'm happy. You only hum when you're happy.

I'm teaching myself to whistle, too. It's not very musical, not like Tommo's, but it's coming. It's coming.

When Tommo arrives we have a few laughs, and together we go over to the classroom. I don't say much, of course. I don't say much to anyone, but it's a start.

'Morning, Georgie,' says Shannon, smiling at me. I get the real ones now instead of the paper ones. Real smiles are even better.

She's always there before me, Shannon, sitting at the table, waiting for things to start. She's busy. She doesn't like to waste time.

'Hi, Shannon,' I say, and I smile back. I don't say a lot more, because I'm a bit shy, especially of girls, and I'm not used to talking, anyway. I'm the quiet type. I think I'll always be the quiet type.

But she doesn't seem to mind. She gets on with her work, chattering away to everyone else. And sometimes she helps me with mine.

I'm watching her. And I'm grateful. Very grateful. Thank you, Shannon. For caring. I never feel angry when you're around, the colours never drain from the world. You're like the stained glass, warming my soul, only more so. When you're close, I'm warm. When you look at me, I'm calm.

I know you're hurting, I know you've been hurting, just like me. But I don't want to think about the past any more, yours or mine. Because it doesn't matter, it doesn't have to matter all the time. Just for once, I want to be Georgie, your friend, here in Wales, fourteen. Not Georgie, little boy, stuck in the past. Not Georgie, bad, lost in the dark.

That's what I want to say to you. When I'm ready. That's what I will say.

And when I've got enough strength maybe I'll be able to reach into the mirror and bring the old Georgie out too, bring him with me into the future. But for now I'm just going to concentrate on me. Just Georgie, here and now, Georgie.

30 may

I was up in my room after school when someone knocked on my door. I always go up there at half past three for a bit of peace and quiet, a bit of space. Sometimes I read. Sometimes I listen to my music. More often I just sit in my chair by the window or lie on the bed and relax. I need it after a full day in school.

I opened the door and there was Tommo. I was a bit surprised. Because we spend all day together I don't often see him out of school any more. I don't need to.

But I could tell by the look on his face it was important. He was holding something, offering it to me. I took it from him and looked at it. It was a photograph.

'I've just been down in the office,' he said. 'Sally gave me this. Said it came in the post this morning, with a load of files from your old school. She thought it might be best to wait until class was over before you saw it.'

A woman and a boy, a young boy. The woman's got long dark hair. She's pushing the boy on a swing in a park. She's standing in front of him so they can watch each other. The boy's smiling, happy, looking straight at his mum. She's smiling too. I can just about make out the sea in the background. Someone's flying a kite down on the beach.

I know who the boy is. It's Georgie. I know who the woman is, too. It's her. The one in my dreams. The one who kisses me awake every morning. Whose face disappears as I wake. The one who's dead.

Tommo puts his arm on my shoulder. 'Are you all right, Georgie?' he says.

Yeah. I'm all right. Sort of.

'Do you want me to leave you on your own?'

Yeah, leave me on my own. Leave me on my own with my mum.

I sit by the window, holding the photo. Sit by the window till the light fades from the sky.

But it doesn't take her away. The daylight can't take her with it, because she doesn't belong to the light any more. She belongs in my mind, comforting me, strengthening me. We were lost, both of us, but we've found each other again, somehow we've found each other.

I don't need to wake in the night any more, crying out for love, because she's out there somewhere, watching over me, loving me.

I'm loved, and now I can love myself. I'm loved, and maybe at last I can begin to love.

15 september

'So what did you think when you saw me tearing lumps out of Bob that day, Georgie? Didn't it put you off me?'

Shannon and Georgie are lying on the grass in the park. They've come in on the Saturday bus trip, and Shannon's showing Georgie how to do one of her famous disappearing tricks.

Georgie sits up, takes a piece of gum out of his mouth and has a good long look at it before answering.

'Yeah,' he says. 'I suppose it did for a while. But it doesn't now. I'm not sure why.'

'Thought it had. But it's OK to be angry sometimes, you know,' says Shannon. 'That's one of the things Tommo's showed me. And you and me, we've a lot to be angry about.'

'Mmm, maybe . . . '

'No maybes about it, kid. It's only normal. It's

part of being human. Being angry's only bad if it takes you over, if you can't escape it.'

'Normal . . . ' says Georgie, rolling the gum between his fingers. 'I don't know what normal is, you know. I'm not sure if I ever will.'

They lie on the grass, Georgie playing with the gum, Shannon blowing smoke rings into the air.

'You know what you were saying about being angry,' says Georgie after a while. 'I've got a mirror in my room. When I was starting to get better I used to think the old Georgie, the angry one, was trapped inside. I used to think I'd have to split myself in two and leave him there. But I don't, do I? He's part of me, and that's OK, isn't it?'

Shannon looks at him, surprised. It's the most she's heard him say. 'Yeah,' she says, nodding. 'Of course it's OK.' And then they both lie back, squinting at the sun.

'You're coming on, aren't you?' says Shannon. 'Making progress.'

'Mmm,' says Georgie, smiling. 'I suppose I am.'

'See that hill up there,' says Shannon after a while. 'Tommo took me there soon after I came to

Abernant. I'd only ever lived in cities before. I stood at the top, looking all around, and I thought it was the most beautiful place I'd ever been.'

'That's funny,' says Georgie. 'He brought me up there too. It was a sunny day, just like today. I can remember him saying to me, "I'd much rather be up here than down in the town, where Shannon went." Funny thing is, I agreed.'

'And would you now?' asks Shannon quietly. 'Would you rather be up there now?'

'No way!' says Georgie, laughing.

'What about the smiley men?' says Shannon a bit later. 'How long did it take you to work out what they meant? Where they came from?'

'I didn't,' answered Georgie. 'I knew they meant cheer up, but I didn't know who was sending them. I didn't understand about the river. Not till Tommo told me.'

'Tommo knows?' says Shannon.

'Of course he knows, silly,' says Georgie. 'He was coming in every morning, days when I was too depressed to even get out of bed. He kept them all safe for me, in the drawer beside my bed.'

'He never said,' says Shannon.

'No,' says Georgie. 'That's because he understood. He knew it was something private, between you and me. He knew it was important.'

'Was it important, Georgie? Important to you?'

'Oh, yes,' says Georgie, nodding. 'It was important all right. If it hadn't been for you, and Tommo of course, I don't know where I'd be now. I don't know who I'd be.'

'Still silent?'

'Definitely.'

'Still trapped behind the mirror?'

'I think so.'

'So Tommo told you I was the river?'

'Yeah,' says Georgie. 'The river Shannon. He says it's in Ireland. Have you ever been there?'

'I was born there,' Shannon answers quietly. 'And I nearly died there, too. I'll tell you about it some time.'

'Hey, we'd better head back to the bus before they send out a search party,' says Shannon quickly. She gets to her feet, stamps out her cigarette, brushes the grass off her jeans and begins to walk, fast.

'Hang on!' cries Georgie, shoving the gum back in his mouth and running after her. 'I don't know the way, remember.'